The Infected Factory

Douglas Rabideau

Published by Rabideau Publishing, 2023.

THE INFECTED FACTORY

First edition. February 14, 2023.

ISBN: 979-8223452812

Written by Douglas Rabideau.

Special thanks to Martin Rabideau for editing

and Luke Rabideau for cover art

"What's this about, Tim? I haven't even finished this month's sales report. There's some outlier data that makes it hard to..." Ryan trailed off as he watched his boss pull an old binder out of his desk drawer.

"Are you familiar with the Legua Database?" Tim was grinning like a maniac. The chair underneath him groaned as he shifted his bulky frame.

"Is that the one from two mergers ago?"

"No, it's even older than that. The password was lost in the documentation—"

"And ten thousand customer contacts were lost with it," Ryan interrupted. "I remember now. Did you find something?"

Tim grinned even wider and opened the binder. "Behold, the password!"

The first sheet inside the binder was yellowed and dirty. Halfway down the page, indented and bolded, was typed:

Matthew Legua's Customer Database
    Username: owner
    Password: password123!

Ryan looked at Tim. "Is this real?"

His boss nodded. "There's a catch, though." He turned his monitor so Ryan could see it. On the screen was the sales database login page, with the Legua Database selected.

At first glance, Ryan knew the login wasn't finished. But the problem wasn't the password. The cause was displayed in bright red at the bottom of the screen:

Your sign-in could not be completed. Please verify access to XXX-XXX-XX85 to continue.

"Multi-factor Authentication. So we need to find the phone number that ends in 85? That's not enough information. It could be anywhere."

"Right. We do have a little more to go on." Tim pointed to a paragraph further down in the binder. "Matthew Legua's number is listed as extension 4985. And the logo at the top belongs to Garret Electronics, one of the companies that merged with us decades ago. We know where their old headquarters are located."

"So you want to find the phone this database is looking for to get access?"

"Exactly. I've talked to the telecommunications division about getting the number ported to a new phone, but this is so old they don't even have it in the system. We'll need to get to the physical location."

Ryan shook his head slowly. "I get that this is some legendary treasure left over from the glory days, but is it really worth anything now? The information inside is over twenty years out of date!"

"Look at it this way. About ten percent of the customers in that database contacted us to update their information. Let's assume another fifty percent have gone out of business or merged with a larger company. Another thirty percent probably have no need of our services after all this time. That leaves ten percent. A thousand viable customers, just waiting to hear from us." Tim leaned back in his chair, ignoring the creaks of strained plastic. "The average customer spends fifteen million a year. If we get in this database, we could be looking at fifteen billion dollars! Imagine the commission on that!"

Ryan grimaced. It was easy to get excited, but he wasn't convinced. "First off, you made those numbers up. How do you know a thousand companies want our products but are too afraid to ask? And second, there's ten thousand contacts. It would take years to go through them all."

"Actually, those estimates are based on atrophy rates in other databases from the same era. I admit, it's impossible to guess the actual numbers. And we would have this entire department running through the contacts. We wouldn't tell them where we got them, and we should be able to run through all ten thousand before any other sales directors find out and want their own slice of pie."

"Like James."

"Ugh. You know what his latest trick is? His entire department is wearing Santa Claus hats! In July! He thinks it will make it easier to get sales if you enter negotiations with a conversation starter. It's backfiring, of course, at the expense of his employee's dignity."

"I'm sure his employees don't have any dignity left. Especially after he was caught sending them to sabotage rival department's lunches."

"Right. For now, we'll just keep this to ourselves. Think about what should be done."

Ryan nodded. "Do you mind if I talk to my friend Quinn about this? You trust him, and he hates James just as much as we do."

"Good idea. Maybe the two of you will think of something."

In the room Ryan and Quinn shared, it only took a few minutes to get Quinn up to speed on the dilemma.

"So," Quinn said, pacing back and forth, "Tim wants to find an old telephone and answer it to get into a mystical database that's twenty years out of date?

"Exactly."

"And he thinks he knows where it is?"

"At the old headquarters for Garret Plastics."

Quinn stopped pacing. "Just to clarify, the reason he talked to you about it instead of calling a security team, is...?"

"Keeping it quiet. This is still owned by Devlin Incorporated, and if it's recovered by Devlin Security, all the sales directors will have equal opportunity to it. This way, only Tim's department will have access."

"But if security doesn't go down there to answer the phone, who is Tim going to send?"

Ryan's expression soured. "We didn't discuss that part, but I imagine he will want to keep the people who know about this to a minimum."

"Meaning: you."

Ryan nodded silently. "Yeah, this is a bad idea."

"But it's fifteen billion dollars."

"Yeah, but my commission is, like, one percent."

"Then, one hundred fifty million dollars."

Ryan's face lit up again.

Quinn sat down and grabbed his tablet, his uncombed brown hair bouncing as he did so. The screen still showed the last login attempt to the database. "Huh. My cell ends in 85. What a coincidence."

He switched programs and typed for a moment. "The Garett headquarters is underneath the Garett-Lasanko factory now, if it still exists at all. That's a lot of area to search, but it might be doable." He frowned. "The GL plant is an old city-factory. It was one of the first fully self-sufficient structures and set the standard for mass production in the decades following."

"Big deal. Half our employees never leave the Tower after getting assigned here."

"Yes, but this was the first to have employees work, eat, sleep, and relax in the same building. At the time, it was because it was literally too large for workers to go home at night and be back the next morning. Now, like the Tower, it's common practice. Garret-Lasanko was only partially automated. I'm not sure why."

Ryan leaned over Quinn's shoulder. "Was this before or after the robot conspiracy in Walmart's Africa plant?"

"I don't remember. That could be why. There aren't many other details on here. It's not on the strategic asset list, and it isn't producing any top selling products." Quinn looked at Ryan. "It's really big. Are you sure you want to go down there?"

"I haven't even decided if I want to go! In fact, I don't want to go!"

"But you do want the money."

They sat in silence for a few moments, until Quinn spoke again.

"Before we decide, I know who can help us. Telephones mean IT, and Fred might have some documentation on the old headquarters. Searching the entire factory is insane. If he has something to narrow it down, we can decide then if it's worth it."

"Right. Don't tell him why we want it, though."

"Of course. I'll be back in a few hours."

Ryan walked through the hallways of Devlin Tower, wandering between the employee housing and the food district twenty floors down. He would get there eventually, but he couldn't stand the crowded elevators. After work hours he usually went to the nearest coffee shop, and enjoyed the view from the floor-to-ceiling windows.

He didn't make it that far today, however. He was busy watching his reflection in the polished walls, and didn't notice the menacing figure in front of him.

"Hey, Sales. Look at me when I'm talking to you."

The voice drew his attention to the speaker, James Gunn. As always, James was dressed in a tuxedo even though the other sales directors only wore suits.

Ryan ignored him and walked past.

"Fine. Lesairo. Wait up."

Ryan kept walking.

James jogged to catch up with him. "I hear your boss has a special project. Watcha working on?"

Ryan kept the surprise off his face. Tim might have let something slip, but he wouldn't be stupid enough to let James have anything serious. "None of your business, Sales."

"Oh, so he does talk! And call me Mister Gunn. I'm not a Sales peon like the rest of you."

"Let's compromise and call you Mister Sales."

James jumped ahead and slammed the wall in front of Ryan. Ryan barely stopped before running into his arm. The HR team might dismiss the conversation as playful banter, but if he ran into someone, even if that someone had intentionally blocked his path, Ryan could get docked for physical harassment.

"Listen here, you low-life." James leaned in close. "I know Tim Garland is doing something, and I will find out about it. If you tell me now, I might have mercy on you. Otherwise, this might be the perfect time to clean house."

Ryan ducked under his arm and continued walking, listening carefully in case James tried to jump in front of him again. Instead, James settled for yelling at him.

"You can't keep secrets from me! You've been a thorn in my side for too long!" With that, James turned and walked the other way.

Once Ryan was sure he was gone, he found the nearest seat and sat down trembling. James picked on everybody, but he had never gone so far before. The coffee shop would have to wait. He headed back to his apartment.

Two hours later, Quinn got back from the IT headquarters wing. "Fred was good for the info. It looks like it might be doable."

"Let's do it, then."

Quinn stopped taking his shoes off and looked at Ryan. "Are you sure?"

There was a gleam in Ryan's eye that took Quinn off guard. "We need to take James down."

"I agree, but surely there's better ways to go about it. I could bribe Fred to look into his message logs for dirt, or something."

"What? You could have done that this whole time?"

Quinn paused. "I didn't think of it 'till now."

"It doesn't matter. Getting the Legua database is how we'll do it. When do we leave?"

"First, we need to look at the plans." Quinn thumbed his tablet and displayed a map of the factory. "Fred didn't have any data on the phone number, but he gave me a couple locations that might have it."

"The phone number?"

"No, data. The phone system is always located in datacenters or server rooms. The system itself won't do us much good, but there should be hardcopy documentation or maps in the same room. Those will point to the exact location of the phone. With the right bribe, he implied he might be able to get us keys to those rooms. They are located here, here, and here." He touched the map in a few places.

"That's pretty far from the entrance."

"These lines are tube trains through the structure. Maybe three hours on rails and another hour of walking once we get inside."

Ryan nodded. "It will take all day to get to the factory, though. We'll need equipment and time off."

"I have off tomorrow. Tim should be able to use his political clout to remove you from duty for a day."

"You have tomorrow off? Why didn't you tell me sooner?"

Quinn shrugged. "I had plans all day. I can cancel them, it's no big deal."

Ryan dug deeper. "What plans?"

"Just plans."

"Was it Christine?"

"No."

"Hanging with Mike?"

"Nope."

"The home game?"

"I'm not going to tell you!"

Ryan pulled up the couch cushion. "So, you were going to stay home in your pajamas and play the new release of Blood War 3?" He picked up the game case and flipped it over. "Rated M for intense violence. I may have to borrow this."

Quinn watched him amusedly. "Yes, I was, but now I'm going to dig through dusty server rooms. Happy?"

"That does make me somewhat happy, yes."

"Alright. See what Tim thinks of this plan."

Surprisingly, Tim approved of their collaboration. Not only that, but he arranged for a Devlin Incorporated helicopter to fly them directly to the entrance. The next morning, they took an express elevator up to the flight deck.

With backpacks in hand, they watched nervously as a red and white helicopter touched down smoothly on the pad outside Terminal C.

An attendant handed them headsets and helped adjust them. "When you step outside, go directly to the helicopter on pad forty-two, and hold a hand-rail wherever possible."

They nodded their understanding. Outside, a light rain was swept across the tall windows by gusts of wind.

The attendant held his hand to his earpiece. "Acknowledged. Passengers in transit." He opened the door and water droplets blew in their face. "Go!"

Outside, the wind whipped their clothes. They pulled themselves along the railing, fearful of letting go and plunging more than a kilometer to the ground.

This flight pad jutted out of the Tower about a hundred meters. It was an odd mix of executive decoration and utilitarianism, with the passenger walkway covered in fancy slip-proof tiles, but maintenance walkways and machinery to the sides were bare metal.

After a minute they reached the end of the railing. The pilot's voice came through their headsets. "Wind is good. Come out on the pad."

After a second of hesitation, they left the railing and sprinted to the helicopter's open door. The flight crew slammed the door shut and some of the noise died down, along with the wind.

"Good morning. My name is Carl Jeski, and I am your pilot today. Our destination is landing pad twenty eight at the GL plant. Flight time will be about two hours."

Ryan fidgeted with the microphone on his headset before strapping himself in. "Hi, Carl. I'm Ryan. What can you tell us about the plant?"

"I'm glad you asked. Just a moment." The pilot flipped a few switches in the cockpit. "This is Oscar Tango Five Zero One to Tower Control. Requesting take-off."

"Oscar Tango Five Zero One, this is Devlin Control. You are clear for take-off on heading six three eight.

"Roger Control, taking off now." The helicopter lifted smoothly into the air, turned to point away from the Tower, and accelerated into the gloomy sky.

"Now, you asked about the GL plant. It's over ten thousand cubic kilometers of factories, warehouses, and offices. As you probably know, that area originally belonged to Garret Plastics before being bulldozed and reconstructed into the Garret-Lasanko factory at the height of the Second Cold War, in the 2030s."

"I'm sorry, the area was bulldozed?" Ryan could hear the worry in Quinn's voice. If the headquarters were demolished, the chances of the phone still existing were low.

"Most of the buildings were destroyed, but the headquarters were built over. There are rumors of a First Cold War bunker under the plant as well. A lot of stuff is hidden under there."

"We're mostly concerned with the headquarters."

"Are you? I could have taken you right there instead of the entrance, but there's a no-fly zone over the plant itself. A hold-over from the Second Cold War. We can enter it in emergencies. Oh, and cell phones won't work inside the factory. You'll need to be on the roof. It's because the roof is reinforced against mortar attacks."

"Mortars? From who?"

"Officially? Terrorists working for China. Unofficially, industrial saboteurs working for Nestle."

"You're kidding!"

"Most people don't know this, but there was never any direct action between the US government and the Chinese government. The biggest players were supercorporations like Disney, Nestle, and Microsoft. The Chinese, as a major factor in the economy, felt they had a stake in the outcome. The US was only involved because a lot of the espionage happened on US soil. They didn't care what happened internationally, like when Disney's Third Atlantic Battle Fleet launched a surprise attack on Microsoft's secret naval base off the coast of Greenland. But when Microsoft Security tried to retaliate by landing a light tank division in Burbank California, the government banned private militaries from entering within fifty kilometers of US territory. That effectively killed the war. If they had waited any longer, it would have gotten a lot bloodier. None of this was reported to the public, of course. Ironically, the US no longer has its own military. They rent private militaries from corporations like ours to maintain order."

"Was Devlin involved in the war?"

"Like a lot of corporations, Devlin Incorporated was waiting on the sidelines for a chance to make it big. Devlin never saw much action, though. Our biggest moment came in 2032 when we acted as a middle-man for the sale of Coca-Cola's secret recipe from Ford Motor Company to Pepsi. We suspect our contact at Pepsi was actually working for Fanta, but we still made an easy billion off of it."

"How do you know all this?"

The pilot banked the helicopter a little to the left while he responded. "You hear a lot of interesting things when you ferry the world's most important people."

"What's the most interesting thing you've heard?"

"That's easy. Nestle has a secret moon base where they experiment with growing exotic foods purchased from space aliens. I don't know I believe it, but it wouldn't surprise me."

They flew in silence for a few minutes. The clouds ahead broke and rays of sunshine lit the smog of the city below them.

"Based on what you heard, how do you think corporations got so powerful?" Ryan asked.

"Capitalist economies are based on business profit. The company who makes circuit boards makes money by selling them to the company who builds computers, who makes money by selling them to other people, including companies that make money selling food to everyone including the first two companies. Everyone nets a little bit of profit in the cycle. If they didn't, they would have to change their business practice or shut down. The supercorporations thought by merging the individual companies together, the profits would rise to the top instead of circulating through the economy. By eliminating the circuit company's profit margin, they could provide circuits to the computer company at cost and the executives could pocket the difference. What they didn't realize, was bigger companies require more overhead. A hundred employees might need an HR department of four or five, but a thousand employees need dozens of HR to keep track of. Even then, a lot of waste happens between departments. Things get overlooked, orders forgotten, products spoiled. There's too much middle management for upper management to get a clear picture of what's happening. The profits the executives thought they would skim off the top are still at the bottom of the economy, but instead of cash it's wasted effort and material." The pilot was silent for a moment. "You're likely to find a lot of that down in GL. Management has been ignoring the problem by literally ignoring the factory, and that only makes it worse. I've overheard the phrase "If it isn't broke, don't fix it" every time an exec brings it up. I don't know exactly what's going on, but stay on your toes."

James Gunn adjusted his bow tie as he entered the IT area. Fred looked up with disinterest.

"May I help you, sir? The help desk is four levels down. This area is off limits to -"

"Do you know who I am?"

Fred's expression didn't change, but he didn't reply either.

James took a step forward. "I am Sales Director Gunn. I go where I please."

The IT worker sat in his chair silently. Jerks like this were common. It was best not to provoke a director, but there was no need to encourage him either.

"I know that dirt stain Ryan Lesairo and his cell-mate Quinn Hammond were up here talking to you. I want to know why."

Fred shrugged. "Actually, I've never heard of this Ryan. Maybe you should try somewhere else."

The director's face went through a few expressions as he realized intimidation probably wasn't going to work. "Fine. I know Hammond talked to you yesterday. If you tell me what's going on, I could make it worth your while." James flashed his million-dollar-smile he usually reserved for board meetings.

Fred's eyebrows perked up. "How?"

"Budget talks are coming up." James looked around the cramped office. "I'm in pretty good with the president, and it looks like it might be in the company's best interest to get you some new equipment." He smiled even wider. "It would be in your best interest, too."

It was a short walk from landing pad twenty eight to the main entrance of the Garret-Lasanko factory building. Tall windows set in the tan walls overlooked the walkway up to revolving doors.

The entrance was crowded, and it took a couple minutes to get inside. The lobby had been beautiful at one point, but it was obvious recent maintenance fell short of what the original craftsmanship intended. A small fountain in the center was bone-dry, and looked like it had been converted to an indoor garden. Now, all it held was decorative dust-covered mulch.

A bank of elevators took them down to the tube train station. The internal network connected most of the building, and some of the surrounding area. A similar network was reserved for cargo.

Ryan and Quinn took seats in the crowded train. The car sped through the tunnels, and they caught an occasional glimpse of factory floors sprawling across the plant, one after the other.

At each station, fewer and fewer people stayed on the train. At their last stop, the terminal was almost deserted.

Ryan patted his pockets to make sure he hadn't left anything on the train. Quinn yawned and stretched his arms. "Three hours on the train. Not looking forward to that again."

"I'm sure there's worse ahead of us." Ryan eyed the worn furniture worriedly. "If we weren't in the middle of a city, I would think this place was abandoned."

"No crowds to fight through." Quinn turned on his tablet, and started walking down one of the hallways. "The decoration is really ugly, though."

Ryan glanced at the fake stone walls as they walked. "Pretty standard for the 2030s, but it would look a lot better if they dusted once a decade or so."

"Get used to it. There's still an hour of walking before we get to the first server room."

An hour later, they were in the general area of their destination. Quinn held the tablet up, twisting it to the side as he tried to read the map.

"We're lost, aren't we?" Ryan sat down on a chair, eyeing the yellowed magazines on the nearby table.

"Not lost, but this junction isn't on the map." Quinn walked down the hall a few meters. "This wall isn't supposed to be here..." After a moment he flipped the tablet around again. "Or maybe it's that wall."

Ryan looked at the navigation signs. "Offices, break room, first aid...I don't see the server room."

"It wouldn't be on there. The IT department is usually the only one to access it."

"How about the break room. Someone there might know where it is."

Quinn looked at Ryan quizzically. "We haven't met another person for twenty minutes. Do you really think anyone is going to be lounging in a lunchroom? It's not even break time."

"Do you have a different idea?"

Quinn shrugged his shoulders and they walked toward the break room.

They opened the doors and looked around. Surprisingly, there were a few dozen people wandering between the vending machines and the tables. They were wearing the old yellow and tan uniforms, a few years behind Ryan and Quinn's blue and tan. All of them looked at the intruders, but most went back to what they were doing after a few seconds.

One man sat alone against the wall, separated from the other employees. His face was hidden in the shadow of a black hoodie, and his dark blue pants stood out from the Devlin Incorporated uniforms. He seemed to stare at them, and Ryan tried not to make eye contact.

Quinn and Ryan cautiously walked further into the room. A shorter man, sitting at a nearby table, watched them intently.

Ryan walked up to him. "Hello sir."

"You gentlemen aren't from around these parts. There somethin' I can help ya with?" The man was polite, though the scowl on his face suggested he'd rather not be. His accent also implied he watched a few too many cowboy movies.

"We're looking for a datacenter nearby. Room DA925-62B?"

Some of the hostility left the man's face, but it was replaced by wariness. "Are ya from management?"

Ryan shook his head. "No, no. We're looking for some IT...stuff." He didn't want to lie and claim to be IT, but the implication would be easier. "We only need to find the server room and we'll be on our way."

"Not many visitors head this way. Not since our late manager disappeared."

"Your manager disappeared?"

"I told ya, he's late. Probably stuck in traffic."

Ryan nodded slowly.

The man continued. "For the last six years."

"Right. Do you know about the server room?"

They stared at each other for a few more seconds. The man finally broke the silence.

"The name's Curtis." He held out his hand and Ryan shook it. "I don't know about 'DA', but you're looking for level 9, section 25, room 62B. You're going to walk out this door, take a left, take a right at the first aid station, and then follow the signs for the stairwell. Level 9 is two levels above us, although the sign might be missin'. Section 25 is about fifteen minutes down the hall, and ya should find room 62B without much trouble."

"Thank you sir!" Ryan and Quinn backed out of the break room.

"Be careful in these here parts," the man called after them. "Ya don't want to find trouble yourself!"

"That was weird," Quinn said. "Did you see that guy with the cloak?"

"Yeah, I did. Let's find the stairwell."

The stairs weren't difficult to find. Curtis' directions were accurate. Although the sign for level 9 was indeed missing, someone had helpfully spray-painted the number on the wall.

Level 9 was dimmer and dustier than the previous level, if that was possible. The grime on the floor suggested that while it might not be abandoned, whoever used this place didn't bother cleaning. The lights that still worked flickered or blinked. The two of them hurried along to section 25.

"This is it. DA925-62B!" Quinn pointed to the room number on a door. "I thought it would be harder to find."

"Harder than six hours of traveling followed by asking suspicious strangers for directions in a deserted wing of a factory?"

Quinn tried one of the keys Fred gave them. "Maybe not. I'm just glad we finally found it." He tried another key and the door swung open.

Filing cabinets, desks, boxes, and piles of paper greeted them inside. They stared at the contents of the supposed data center.

Ryan broke the silence. "Are there supposed to be computers in here?"

"Yeah." Quinn picked up a paper and studied it.

"Could this be an IT storage room, or something?"

"No, I don't think so. These papers are from accounting." He tossed the paper back on its pile. "Anyway, I don't think this room was ever a datacenter. All this stuff has been here a while. The walls I can see don't have enough power outlets, there's no data cables coming in, and no marks on the floor from server racks."

"Could Curtis have given us the wrong directions?"

Quinn looked at the room number on the door, then at his tablet. "No, this is the right room. There's just no servers here."

"Now what? Should we find the next room?"

Quinn sighed. "I don't like this. We clearly have bad intel, and the environment here is a lot worse than I thought. I say we head back to the Tower and do some more research before we try again."

Ryan nodded. "You're right. But first, I'm hungry and I saw a Ferino's vending machine in the break room."

"You want to go back there? After the creepy stares we got? Besides, we have food in our backpacks."

"I know, but I already ate three granola bars on the way here and I can't stand another six hours without some decent food."

"Ugh, fine. Ferino's does sound good. But eat fast. I don't want to be in this building any longer than I have to."

"Agreed."

Anticipating the stares, Ryan and Quinn walked quickly to the vending machine, made their purchase, and sat down to a hurried meal. At least the cloaked stranger was no longer there, but they were interrupted halfway through by Curtis.

"Did ya find what you were after, gentlemen?"

Quinn shook his head. "Thanks for the directions, but what we wanted wasn't there."

"And so ya came back here?"

Ryan pointed at his sandwich. "Cause we were hungry."

Curtis frowned as if he were disappointed. "I've tried to impress on you gentlemen that this is not a safe place to be."

They were suddenly aware of a dozen people in dirty, worn uniforms surrounding the table. A little too close to be onlookers. Ryan put down his sandwich. "We're not looking for trouble. We'll be heading out just as soon as we finish eating."

"Now, see, I already gave ya that option. And yet, you're back 'ere for more."

Quinn slowly stood up. "What do you mean? What's going on?"

"You're not wearing the Devlin Incorporated colors." Curtis pointed to his own awful combination of yellow and tan. "You don't belong here."

"Actually, if you'll look here," Quinn held up his badge, "you'll see we are indeed with Devlin Inc. We're all on the same side here."

The short man scowled. "Ain't never seen a red badge before. And your blue shirt is suspect too. If ya ask me, I'd say you look almost squinty-eyed. Now, if y'all will come quietly, we'll hand ya over to the proper authorities without too much fuss."

Ryan's heart was pounding, but that didn't stop him from cramming the last of his sandwich in his mouth. "Yeth. We thurender." He held up his hands. Quinn looked at him oddly, but did the same.

Most of the people around the table relaxed, and some even drifted away. But Curtis' eyes gleamed. "Right this way, if you please." He led them out of the break room, but Ryan noted only two people followed them. The rest were sitting around the tables, reading yellowed magazines.

They turned a few corners, which gave Ryan the time to finish swallowing the last of his sandwich. He caught Quinn's eye and nodded. Simultaneously, they grabbed Curtis' shoulders and threw him back into the other two employees. They ran down the hall, ignoring cries to stop. Further away, they heard the break room doors burst open as more people joined the pursuit.

Ryan tried to remember the path to the train terminal, but they hit a dead end. Footsteps just down the hall jolted them into action. He grabbed a door handle and pulled. Locked.

"Try the other side!" He hissed to Quinn. Together, they tried half a dozen doors before they found one that was unlocked.

They tumbled inside and quietly closed the door. Rows of desks with computer screens greeted them, dark and unused.

Quinn pushed the lock lever. From the hall, footsteps went back and forth. The door handle wiggled as someone tried the latch from the other side.

They put their ears to the door.

"They must o' come this way!" Curtis' voice.

"Ain't no sign o' them. All the doors are locked."

"Could they have doubled back and headed for the terminal?"

"If they did, they'll find Aaron and Johnnie guarding it. Aaron, any sign of them?"

A radio squacked, but Ryan couldn't make out what was said.

"Ya really think they're Chinese, Curtis?"

"If not Chinese, then they belong to corporate, or the McKay's, an' I dunno which is worse. You saw their outlandish clothing."

"Ya should have captured them soon as they walked in, Curtis. Should we bring in Security this time?"

"And ya mother should o' aborted you when she had the chance, Grant. Those brutes ask too many questions and poke their noses where they don't belong. We'll handle this ourselves."

The voices faded away. Ryan and Quinn looked at each other in the darkness. "The train is being guarded. Now what?"

Quinn thought for a few seconds. "We could try making it to the roof."

"And then what? Walk to the helicopter pad?"

The tablet came out and Quinn pulled up the map. "The next nearest terminal is about two hours away on foot."

"But how do we get there? They probably have sentries on all the main hallways and stairwells!"

"We don't know that, and we can't stay here. There's no cell reception, we only have seven granola bars left between us, and I didn't finish my sandwich!"

Ryan nodded slowly. "But they have radios, too. They're organized."

"So are we. We've got a map. We just need to find a safe exit strategy."

The loading dock was quiet. Quinn looked around cautiously, and motioned for Ryan to follow. Half crouched, Ryan ran to the next piece of cover.

An echo sounded through the empty space. It sounded like a barrel fell over. Both of them dropped down out of sight.

The echoes passed. After a minute, they looked up and scanned the dock again.

On one side of the concrete platform, three sets of train tracks passed from the near tunnel, under an overhead crane, and into the far tunnel. On the other side of the platform, a jumble of offices and side rooms crowded the wall. The platform itself was littered with shipping containers, crates, and trash.

"Do you see anyone?"

"No. I think we're clear."

Quinn ran ahead to the next shipping container while Ryan watched the rear. Nothing seemed amiss, and Quinn gave the all clear signal.

They crept between the container and the office. Their advance was interrupted by a sudden noise behind them.

Startled, they turned to see a lady in her fifties inside the office. She tapped on the window again. "Hello. Can you help me?"

Ryan wiped the dust off his shirt and did his best impression of someone who hadn't been sneaking around on a loading dock. "Who are you? What do you need help with?"

"I'm Kena. I'm from the McKay's. You don't seem to be from around here."

"Uh, no, we're not. What do you need?"

"Well, you see, I was working in the plant, in section 137, when a group of Landonites came up and made me come back with them. They're keeping me here for ransom. Can you help me get out of here?"

"Ah..." Ryan glanced at the door. The overhead crane had been used to drop a shipping container in front of the door, trapping Kena inside. "I'm sorry. There isn't anything we can do right now, but we'll come back for you!"

"Oh, thank you!"

Quinn leaned in to whisper to Ryan. "What do you mean, we?"

Ryan whispered back. "Naturally, not us, but a security team."

An alarm blared, making both of them jump. Yellow lights mounted in the ceiling lit up and rotated. As they watched, one person in the near tunnel ran out in the open, and another in the far tunnel hid in an alcove. The alarm sounded again. A whisper of wind echoed through the tunnel, quickly rising in intensity until it sounded like a jet engine. Suddenly, a cargo train sped through the dock. It was moving too fast to see any details, and after a few seconds it was past. The noise died down again, and Ryan and Quinn ducked down to avoid the guards.

"Do you think they saw us?" Ryan's face was flushed from adrenaline.

"I don't think so. But it doesn't matter. We're not going to walk along the rails."

Ryan risked a peak at the two men in the tunnels. "Hide! One of them's coming this way!"

"In the shipping container!" Quinn pointed to the open door of a container next to them. The woman in the office waved goodbye as they closed the door.

They both took a couple deep breaths. Ryan pulled his cell phone out and turned on the flashlight. "Maybe we can just wait in here for the next freight delivery."

"I suppose it could work. What are they shipping, anyway?"

Ryan examined a crate until he found the shipping code. He scanned it with his phone. "This is weird. These are type 47 circuit boards. We haven't used type 47 for years!"

"Maybe they're legacy parts. For old electronics we still have to support."

"No, I'm certain everything with type 47 is out of support. I'm a salesman, I know what we sell."

Quinn frowned. "Could this crate just be left over from the last decade?"

Ryan looked at his phone again. "This label was created two days ago."

"But they would need to be getting parts from somewhere. Who is still sending parts for a decommissioned product? And where are they sending them?"

"It says section 109, still in the GL plant. I don't know what that means, though."

"An entire assembly line is producing items we no longer sell. It's either corruption, or mismanagement."

"Their manager has been missing for six years. I'm guessing they never got the message to stop the machines. The helicopter pilot told us there were inefficiencies, but I never imagined an entire assembly line could get lost in the system like this."

"So what now?" Quinn sat down on a crate. "This shipping container has been waiting for pickup for two days. It could take days more until it gets loaded onto a train, and even when we arrive, whoever unloads it could be in league with Curtis."

"You're right. We need to find a new route. I think we should backtrack and get out of this loading dock."

Quinn nodded. He pushed the door open enough to stick his head out. "I think the coast is clear. Cover me."

He ran between the office and the other shipping containers. The old lady was still at the window, watching them.

Ryan crept out and prepared to run across the open distance when the lady tapped on the glass and pointed behind him. Leaning around the corner of the container, he saw a worker running toward them across the tracks.

Ryan abandoned caution and ran. The worker yelled something, and Quinn looked up.

"Run!" He passed Quinn and both of them rushed toward the exit. Ryan tried to pull down a stack of crates in front of the door, but they were full and he wasted valuable seconds trying to move them.

The other guard saw them, but they were still thirty meters behind. Ryan slammed the door to the dock and ran down the hallway.

"Which way?"

"Doesn't matter! We need to lose them!" They turned left just as the door behind them burst open.

A couple turns later, they felt safe enough to slow down. Ryan listened for following footsteps. The pounding of his heart made it difficult.

"What now?"

Quinn took a few breaths before he answered. "I have no idea. But we need to keep moving."

Ryan nodded and together, they turned a corner.

They were confronted by the hooded stranger from the break room. "I've been looking for you." They turned to run.

"Wait!" He pulled his hood down, revealing short hair and a goatee. "My name is Alex. I'm here to help you."

"Who are you?"

Alex unzipped his hoodie and revealed the dark blue uniform underneath. "I work for Ferino's vending company. I restock the machines in the lunchrooms. More importantly, I can get you back to Devlin Tower where you belong."

"How do you know we're from the Tower?"

"You're wearing the updated company dress code. Only loyalists have access to that. And, your badges are red. That means Tower personnel. First ones I've seen, but I know enough to recognize it."

"Loyalists?"

Alex listened for a second. "They're coming. We need to hurry." Without waiting to see if they followed, he jogged down the corridor.

Ryan and Quinn looked at each other before the sound of footsteps behind them spurred them into action.

"What's going on here?" He asked Alex, but the man just shook his head. "Save your breath. You'll need it."

The three of them passed through nearly a kilometer of hallways, warehouses, and maintenance tunnels. Finally, they stopped in a stairwell.

Ryan leaned on a railing to catch his breath. "So, where are we going?"

"Curtis will try to imprison you as long as he can. You can't escape through his territory."

"But where are we going?"

Alex sat down, panting for air. "McKay territory, the Landonite's rivals. The Landonites are Curtis' group." He cleared his throat and continued. "The McKay's are more reasonable, but Curtis sees you as a threat. He has his own cult down here, and he knows if his department is reintegrated with the loyalists, he will lose all the power he has. That, or get downsized. He thinks you're a spy for HR."

"Why are you helping us?"

"I'm not a terribly nice person, but Curtis has a tendency to lock people up and only release them when his demands are met or it gets expensive to feed them. You don't deserve that sort of treatment, and you don't know enough to survive down here on your own. I'll escort you as far as I can.

"I've gained a lot of traction advertising myself as neutral. Both Landonites and McKays need to eat, so they've allowed me to pass through their battle lines. Smaller groups too, the ones that keep their heads down, always welcome me. I spend most of my time working in the loyalist sections, of course. But when I can I explore the plant for more groups to sell my merchandise to. Other vendors want this territory, even from Ferino's, and I need to make sure everyone wants to buy from me."

"That's kind of like what I do," Ryan said. "Our jobs are really similar."

"Yeah." Alex stood up "Come on. It's not much further." He started down the stairs.

"Hold on. Wouldn't it be better to go to the roof?"

"This stairwell doesn't go to the roof. There aren't many that do."

Ryan and Quinn followed him down the stairs. "What do you mean by loyalist?"

"Departments still loyal to the Tower. None of the people decided to secede from the company, but without contact from management, most don't have any choice. As long as they keep getting paid, they stay here and follow the last orders they were given. Corporate living quarters still work, and there's plenty of shelter. A lot of groups rely on me for food, but some grow or even hunt their own."

"Hunt?"

Alex looked back at them as they walked downward. "I'm not sure what. But nature always reclaims what man abandons. Some sections have been abandoned longer than others." He stopped at a door. "The

McKays are just beyond here." He pushed the door open and walked through.

Instantly, a bright light blinded them. "Stop right there! Identify yourselves!"

Alex raised his hands. "Alex, from Ferino's vending. These are my friends."

Ryan could barely make out shapes moving behind the searchlight pointed at them. One of them approached and roughly patted them down. At their insistent tugging, he reluctantly allowed them to search his backpack.

"Suspects are clean. Kill the light."

As his eyes adjusted to the normal lighting, he saw four people in the hallway. They wore the same yellow and tan dress code as the Landonites, but a red sash was tied around their left arms.

One of them, a tall woman with dark red hair, stepped forward. "Who are you and why shouldn't we arrest you right now?" Her stance seemed militant, and now that he noticed, all four of them held themselves with a disciplined air.

Alex spoke for them. "They're Tower employees. We're just passing through to the train terminal."

The woman looked at the two of them suspiciously. "What are Tower personnel doing down here?"

"We were trying to find some documents from before a merger, but now we just want to get out."

"If your documents are this far down, they may as well be lost."

Quinn nodded. "That's become obvious. Our priority now is getting back to the Tower."

"You're aware you're headed in the opposite direction?"

Alex put his hands down. "They're running from the Landonites. Curtis has locked down all the transportation in his territory. This was the only direction we could go in."

The woman raised her eyebrow. "That does give you some points, but we'll need more than that to give you free passage."

"Come on Mary, you know how Curtis treats his prisoners. They wouldn't stand a chance."

"Shut up, Alex. Landonites took one of our workers just last week, and he's demanding our last air compressor for her return. We can't operate without compressed air! How can I ransom a prisoner if there's nothing for her to come back to?"

"You mean Kena?"

Everyone looked at Ryan. Mary took a step forward. "Yes, her name is Kena. Did you see her?"

"Yeah, she's at the loading dock. She seemed uninjured..." He was cut off by Mary turning to one of the other guards.

"Chester! Assemble a strike team. Make a feint at their storehouse while Hanson and Smith infiltrate the loading dock. Don't take prisoners, just extract the hostage."

"Yes ma'am!" The guard turned on his heel and left the room.

Mary turned back to Ryan. "If your intel is good, you'll be welcome here as long as you need. In the meantime, you'll be treated to our finest guest quarters. Please follow me."

The employee housing claimed by the McKay faction was worn, but clean. While Curtis and the Landonites claimed large chunks of territory without maintaining it, the McKays protected a smaller but better groomed section.

Ryan paced back and forth on the faded carpet. Alex watched him glumly. "You should save your strength. We have a lot of walking ahead of us."

Ryan shrugged, but slowed his steps. "Why are you here? I thought the McKay's liked you."

"They do. I can leave whenever I want. I'm just keeping you guys company. You know, I was trying to keep you guys neutral. It can be dangerous to take sides."

Ryan stopped pacing. "What was I supposed to do? Just let her rot in that office?"

"These guys talk a big game, and I think the McKays go a little overboard with their military play-acting, but no one ever gets hurt."

Quinn nodded. "Now that I think about it, neither group was ever carrying a weapon."

"Right. Skirmishes are decided by intimidation, not violence. They start brawling occasionally, but the only medicine available is through me. The vending machines don't offer anything more advanced than first aid. The hospital section is controlled by an isolationist group. They'll treat outsiders but it costs a pretty penny. The only other medical treatment is Devlin Security, but that gets reported to the Tower. Reports mean inspections. Even Mary wants to avoid that." He rose from the chair and stretched his legs. "Not only that, but if this became a warzone, I think they know I would stop doing business with them. This place is dangerous, but I'm not getting paid enough to carry a weapon."

"Plus, there's a 'no weapons allowed on premises' sign on the entrance," Quinn helpfully pointed out.

"Oh yeah, all twenty kilometers from here. I'm sure everyone remembers seeing that on their first day of work."

"But how would they get weapons? The only imports they get are through the vending machines."

"You forget we're sitting in the middle of a giant factory. They could scavenge enough parts and machinery to build a battle tank if they knew how. Even without any chemical knowledge, if you take a battery and a small compressor, stick it in a backpack, and have a pellet hopper feed into a tube with a trigger activated valve, you have yourself a very heavy but reasonably accurate air-powered automatic weapon. You don't need a range greater than 30 meters for close quarters."

"Huh." Ryan tossed himself on the bed. "But what about Curtis' boss? He said their manager disappeared six years ago."

"Missing doesn't mean injured. He's probably holed up in a middle-management apartment, collecting his paycheck and submitting bogus reports. I wouldn't worry about it. People go missing all the time down here." He glanced at Ryan. "I realize that's not as reassuring as I meant it to be."

Quinn leaned forward. "Do you have any idea why Curtis is sending type 47 circuit boards to section 109?"

"Type 47...109..." Alex thought for a moment. "As a matter of fact, I do. Section 109 is an internal shipping hub for the factory, but it's close to the recycling center. It's on my route, and I recall seeing crates of type 47s being marked for recycling with other outdated products. After breaking down the materials, they're sent back into the supply chain to be made into more products. I suppose that includes more type 47s."

Ryan wrinkled his forehead. "Does Curtis know they're wasting their time?"

"I suspect so. I hadn't put the details together before now, but I think the shipping manager in section 109 knows as well. I doubt they're in league with each other. They're probably just following their last orders. But their alternative is to admit they're as obsolete as the product itself. This way, all their people are still employed and busy, and the managers stay in power. Mary seems too earnest to go along with that sort of scam. But I honestly don't know whether her crates end up in section 109. Even if they do, I don't know if there's a better way. These people don't have much choice."

Just then, the door opened and Mary walked in. They all stood to their feet.

"Good news. Kena's back safe and sound, and we didn't lose any of our men busting her out. But I'm sure Curtis will guess how we knew where to look for her. You boys best get going, but you're welcome here any time."

"Thank you, ma'am."

"Please, call me Mary. And be careful out there. Not everyone is as friendly as us. Where are you taking them, Alex?"

"The train terminal on the fifth level."

"That spur has been disconnected for years. There's one train there, but even if it still ran, the tunnels are blocked off. We don't even guard it anymore."

Alex nodded. "I know. I'm hoping the direct line in the train director's station still works."

"It doesn't. All the power in that section is dead. Not even analog phone lines are working there."

"Bummer. That only leaves one option."

Mary nodded silently. Ryan and Quinn watched with growing apprehension.

Alex turned to the Tower employees. "I hope you're rested up. The only way out is down, through the sub-levels."

The McKay soldiers left them in another stairwell. They started down, listening to the echoes of their footsteps.

"This is one of six stairwells that go down to the basement, or more commonly called the sub-level. One of them is in Landonite territory, but Mary said she had a team sweep the perimeter and they didn't detect any activity."

"That's reassuring. Are you sure you can trust her?"

"This time, sure. She's tried to 'creatively negotiate' with me a couple times in the past. But unlike Curtis, eager to build his empire without Tower interference, she wants management to find her loyally upholding the tenants of Devlin Incorporated. She knows her employee handbook is ten years out of date, so aiding you is the best way to prove her worth to the Tower. That assumes the Tower ever discovers or cares about what's going on down here."

"I can't believe they wouldn't care, but how can this even happen?"

"That's the way life is here. Imagine the corporation is like a body. The departments are organs. When everything does what it's supposed to, everyone benefits. But if one of the organs gets sick, or infected, everyone suffers. Now, the departments in this part of the factory have been cut off. No matter how sick they are, Devlin is redundant and bloated enough that it doesn't notice that some if it's organs are infected. Not to mention missing."

They finally reached the bottom. Alex struggled with the latch on the door. "It's not supposed to be locked. If someone got locked out there, they could die pretty easily." With a moan of rusted metal, the door suddenly swung open.

A blast of hot, dry air flooded the stairwell. Ryan and Quin stepped into the sub-level, staring in every direction.

Concrete pillars, spaced ten meters apart, continued into the distance as far as they could see. Seven meters above, the ceiling was a grid of concrete girders stretched between pillars. These were covered in pipes, cables, ducts, and wires. Most were strapped in place, but some drooped or dangled low to the floor. Incandescent lights gave the space a warm glow. But fully half of them had gone out, and the room was a patchwork of light and darkness.

The floor was covered in dust. No boxes or crates, not even trash broke the expanse of dust. Some places looked to be three or four centimeters deep.

Ryan and Quinn slowly walked further into the sublevel, looking at all the nothingness. The door slammed behind them, and Alex led them into the ocean of dust.

Narrow paths led in different directions. Alex started down one. "Don't step outside the path. If the Landonites are following, extra tracks will lead them right to us."

Ryan eyed a motorcycle leaning against the stairwell wall. The engine was missing and the frame was covered in the same dust. "Why is this place so empty?"

"I think, when the plant was first built, there was a rule against storing things here. When management in the building degraded to the point no one cared, there were plenty of empty and more convenient rooms. The sub-level is almost fifty kilometers wide, and there are only six entrances. That makes it rather useless unless you are traveling from near one entrance to someplace near another. The shortest distance is a straight line, something you can't usually achieve in the factory above."

It seemed they walked for hours, but time was impossible to gauge in the sunless desert. It was mostly silent, but the humming and clunking of distant machinery echoed from one pillar to another until it was a quiet, constant drone.

Ryan noticed the blanket of dust wasn't uniform. In some places the concrete was almost bare, and in others the dust rose to peaks of a few centimeters. The shapes reminded him of something, but he couldn't pin it down until an awful stench stopped him in his tracks. Looking up, he saw an open duct almost a meter wide. It was gently blowing a breeze smelling of trash and decay. As he stared, he thought he caught a glimpse of eyes staring back at him. If there was something there, they vanished before he got a better look. He hurried to catch up with Alex and Quinn.

Dunes, he thought. The breeze from the ducts create air streams, which carve the dust into dunes. He sniffed the air. After the overwhelming smell of dust, he could still detect traces of whatever had been in that duct. Every vent down here must be filled with the same thing.

They came to an intersection. Alex glanced around, as if looking for a landmark, and chose another path. Ryan looked for a marker, but nothing unique appeared in the uniform forest of concrete. They could have been walking in circles for all he knew. He looked behind him, where the stairwell should be. The distance was swallowed up in long lines of pillars.

For a while longer, nothing eventful happened. They continued in single file, Alex leading, followed by Quinn, and Ryan taking the rear.

Suddenly, Ryan tripped. He plunged into the dust and sneezed violently. A billowing cloud marked his impact. Alex stopped and carefully moved past Quinn.

Ryan would have sneezed again, but Alex grabbed his shoulder and pulled him up. "We need to move. Hurry."

The echoes of Ryan's sneeze still bounced through the dry air. But instead of fading away, it was replaced by another sound. Ryan's blood ran cold and he ran to keep up with Alex.

"What is that?"

"We don't know. It's easy enough to avoid, but no one has ever seen it up close. At least, they didn't live to tell about it."

A whisper, more organic than machine, resonated through the half-lit space. It seemed to come from every direction. Slowly, it grew louder. Ryan could swear it was coming from behind them.

"At least we don't have to worry about being followed!" Alex laughed softly. "Whatever it is, it doesn't leave tracks, but the dust is scattered. It will take weeks to form the paths again."

"Bats, maybe?"

"Could be. Even probably."

"But bats don't eat humans."

"That we know of. If you want to wait here and ask it when it catches up to you, be my guest." Alex increased his speed.

It could have been a trick of the light, but the incandescent lights behind them seemed to dim. Ryan could imagine a swarm of thousands of wings rushing toward them with unknown purpose. The whisper grew louder.

Ahead of them, nothing but pillars met his gaze. His breathing was heavy, and he knew there was no point in asking where they were going. Alex knew the way.

The echoes made it impossible to determine the direction of the threat. Ryan kept looking back, but nothing solid materialized. After a while, he wasn't even sure the ominous murmur was getting louder. But with a start of panic, he realized it was.

Still nothing in front of them. Alex stopped suddenly and Ryan almost ran into Quinn. Set flush with the floor were a set of metal doors. Alex grabbed one side and Quinn grabbed the other. With a groan, the doors slowly swung upwards. Concrete steps led down and vanished in the darkness.

"Get in! Quickly!"

Despite the lack of light, Ryan and Quinn wasted no time rushing part way down the stairs. If anything, the echoes from above were even louder down here.

Alex looked back one more time and, with a mighty heave, pulled the doors shut.

The dull gray walls and ceiling of the maintenance tunnels were covered in cables and pipes. Pale blue lights dotted the corridors. The lights at intersections and points of interest were still on, but at the expense of lesser used passageways. Empty sockets left much of the second sub-level in darkness. It was down these paths Alex led the Tower employees.

Quinn ran his finger over a railing and checked it for dust. "It doesn't look like anyone was here recently."

"No. These tunnels aren't as useful for traveling," Alex said. "There are a few outposts down here, but they're mostly safe havens for scavengers and rogues."

"What do they scavenge?"

"Old equipment. Older than what's available up above. Some of the storerooms here have thick doors and heavy locks, and the more industrious scavengers think they're close to a fortune."

"But what are they looking for?"

Ahead, the passage intersected a deep pit. Dim light from above showed a grated bridge crossing the ten meter hole. The light didn't reach the bottom.

Alex raised his voice to be heard above the echoes of their footsteps on the grating. "A way out. Almost every faction is willing to buy or trade valuable equipment, and everyone still has access to their external banking accounts. If someone struck it rich, they could afford to leave this place."

"But if they're selling Devlin property, even internally, wouldn't they get in trouble with corporate?"

"As I understand it, if Devlin tried to sue they would have to acknowledge all this was happening inside their own land. Your billion dollar legal department could probably sink you in court regardless. More practically, everyone and everything in the abandoned sections have been lost in the system. Devlin has no official record and couldn't prove ownership even if they knew it was being traded. Besides, it's all staying in the GL plant, and being used by Devlin employees."

"So their paychecks are automated? What about the IRS?"

"That's a good point. You're the first Tower employees I've met, but I've discovered an outpost or two by helping IRS agents track down someone who missed a figure in their taxes. Devlin Incorporated may have forgotten, but the IRS knows exactly how many people work here."

The passageway narrowed. Large pipes stretched across the path, and they had to stoop or crouch underneath.

"I can't believe people live like this. These conditions are terrible!"

"It's true, an abandoned factory isn't much of a place to live. But there's shelter, power, and heat. As long as you don't mind vending machine food, you have everything you need to stay for years."

"But it's dangerous! People get kidnapped, and what was that in the basement? I don't think bats are the answer."

Alex stopped. "You're right, I don't think it was bats. And people do disappear. We're on the edge of something, between civilization and the great unknown. And the unknown is growing. Let me show you something." With that he took off, through empty passageways, steam-filled rooms, tunnels half blocked with rubble, and doorways hidden in darkness. Finally, they stopped at a vending machine.

Alex turned off his flashlight as he approached. The light from the machine was the only illumination in the tunnel. "Cora's Cola" was printed in big wavy letters on the front. Every flavor was out of stock, except one.

Quinn shook his head. "Cora's has been out of business for ten years! Did you inherit this?"

"Twelve years. And it's not mine."

"So...they left a vending machine down here? Even in its heyday, the GL plant wouldn't have had enough workers walking through this tunnel to justify putting a machine here."

"This wasn't part of the GL plant." They both turned to look at Alex. "This was Garret Plastics."

"Garret Plastics? This is the headquarters?" Ryan looked around the tunnel. Behind the tangle of pipes and wires, the concrete of other tunnels was replaced by faded wallpaper.

"No, this was one of the satellite offices. When they built the GL plant, they just built on top of this one. The offices were used for a few more years. Eventually, in one remodel or another, this became a maintenance tunnel. The rooms nearby still have filing cabinets filled with legal documents labeled 'Do not dispose for thirty years'."

"Wow." Ryan nodded sadly. "But why show us the vending machine?"

Alex took three quarters from his pocket and inserted them into the coin slot. He pushed the flavor for vanilla three times, and three Cora's Cola vanilla-flavored soda bottles rolled out.

"You're kidding! It still has Cora's Cola in it? These could be worth a fortune as collector's items!"

"Yes, and if the average scavenger got his hands on this, that's exactly what he would think. But I know better." Alex opened his bottle and took a sip. "These bottles haven't aged. Not that you can tell, anyway. There's no expiration date."

Quinn twisted his bottle, looking for a date. Ryan shrugged and swallowed a gulp of cola. "So there's no date. What of it?"

"All soda manufactured is required to have an expiration date. But that's not the weirdest thing. These machines hold 48 bottles in each slot. As far as I know, I am the only person who knows about this place. Since I found it, I have purchased at least twice that number, and it is still stocked."

Ryan swallowed slowly. "That's impossible."

A grin spread across Alex's face. "I know."

Quinn looked at the sides of the machine. "Have you tried to open it?"

"The lock is different. I should be able to open it, but none of my keys fit. The lock is worn, however. What that means is anyone's guess."

Ryan tapped the plastic on the front. "We could break it open."

"No! If you were the owner of this machine, trying to keep a piece of history alive, how would you feel if someone just bashed apart your legacy? And even if there was an answer to the puzzle, some obscene factory producing an endless supply of ancient soda, what then? Exploit it for profit?"

The salesman shook his head. "I didn't think of that."

"My point is, sometimes it's best not to question the magic. I can't explain what the thing is in the first sub-level, and I can't explain this. Maybe I should try to understand them better, but I'm afraid if I look too closely I'll break the magic."

"But there must be some explanation!"

Alex shrugged. "Devlin Incorporated may own the place, but they left it long ago. The destinies of the people Devlin abandoned have been inherited by something else. Something growing at the heart of the factory. Whether aliens, demons, fairies, rainbow-puking unicorns or nothing but figments of our own imagination, we may never know. But it isn't completely hostile. This machine is proof of that."

Ryan and Quinn looked at each other. "I think you're making too much of a magic vending machine."

"Maybe. Maybe. But you asked me to explain it. I think while there is a perfect explanation, it might not be found in our lifetime. If ever."

Quinn downed the last of his cola. "I can live with that."

Their guide screwed the top onto his own half-full bottle and put it in his pocket. "It's not much further to the flooded sections. There aren't many humans down here, but keep your guard up."

A small scavenger party met them a while later. Far from hostile, they wanted to trade and were disappointed when Ryan and Quinn had little to offer. Despite that, the scavengers gifted a small figurine to both of them. It was roughly machined out of steel, and bore little resemblance to any living creature but was still artistic and beautiful. Later, Alex supposed they wanted to gain the Tower's favor. Ryan and Quinn supposed Alex was envious.

Not much further on, they entered the flooded sections. A third, deeper sub-level was filled with half a meter of water. Alex wasn't sure where it came from, but the water rose over the years.

THE INFECTED FACTORY

The flooded areas were not hard to negotiate. They simply stayed one level up. The maintenance tunnels were left behind, and they entered factories, warehouses, and offices once again. This stage of the journey was uneventful, until they entered factory D118.

Ryan immediately knew this place was different by the echo. There were many wide spaces in the GL plant, but this one had an unusual sound.

Only a handful of the hundreds of overhead lights still worked. The doorway they entered from spilled light into the huge space. Hulks of rusted machinery towered above, all but invisible in the darkness. Below, as still as a mirror, oily water covered the floor.

Their path turned and twisted among the machinery. Catwalks and walkways extended from one wall to the other, climbing and descending in a maze. Their exit was visible as a distant light in the murky darkness.

Again, Alex chose a path without hesitation. Ryan and Quinn followed close behind.

Their guide glanced at them over his shoulder. "I know this looks intimidating, but this path is relatively well traveled. As long as you stay on it, there shouldn't be any danger." He swept the beam of his flashlight around them, briefly giving shape and detail to the shadowy machines nearby.

Quinn pulled out his cellphone and turned on the flashlight. Ryan left his in his pocket, afraid of dropping it in the water.

Slowly, they walked through the artificial cavern. Some of the walkways were blocked or damaged, but Alex always guided them to safe passage.

Idly, Quinn picked up a broken pipe and threw it into the water. Alex jumped at the sound and pointed his light at the source.

"What happened?"

"It was just me. I threw something in the water."

Small waves radiated from the splash to gently lap at the sides of the machinery. Large bubbles rose from the spot.

Ryan nudged Quinn, a little harder than he needed to. "I wish you wouldn't disturb the water. Who knows what could be hiding there?"

Alex stared at the bubbles, but shook his head. "There's nothing in the water. Too much oil. Some places have fish, but I've known this place for four years and I've never seen or heard of anything living here." All the same, he looked just as concerned as Ryan.

They continued their trek. They just finished climbing a ladder to another catwalk, twenty meters above the floor, when Alex stopped.

"Is something wrong?" Ryan asked.

Alex shone his flashlight at the mangled grating in front of them, and then across the void left by the missing walkway. Four meters away, the rest of the walkway continued into the blackness. "The path is broken. We can't go this way."

They shone their lights around, searching for another route. Overhead cranes cast eerie shadows as far as the light could reach.

"Let's backtrack. There's another way, although I don't know if it's safe." Alex squeezed past them to take the lead.

The secondary path was only a few minutes away. This one was much closer to the water, only five meters above. Quinn shone his light at the colorful oil patches.

"How deep is the water?"

"About a meter. You can stand up if you fall in, but that's obviously not recommended. Aside from the oil, there's a lot of tools and objects hidden on the floor."

"The bubbles from earlier looked a lot deeper."

"There are machinery pits in the floor. I think there was one where Quinn threw something."

Ryan didn't think Alex was very confident in that answer. But like the vending machine from earlier, he decided it was best not to question it and escape as soon as they could.

Their new route took them along the spine of a huge piece of machinery. It wound past control stations, open electrical boxes, and hatches leading to deep spaces. Flecks of blue paint among the rust testified the long gone glory days of the factory.

Quinn swept his light behind them. Ryan followed it with his eyes, still keeping his own in his pocket. Suddenly he grabbed Quinn's arm.

"What was that?" He pointed in the darkness where Quinn's light had just been.

Alex turned around, keeping his flashlight low. "What was what?"

"I thought I saw something." Ryan fumbled with his cellphone before getting it out of his pocket and turning on the flashlight. He aimed it at the dark.

"They're just pipes."

"Three pipes. I thought I saw another one, and it was green. Not rusty."

A splash, so faint they weren't sure they heard it, came from close by. Instantly, they pointed their lights downward and searched the water. Not even a ripple showed itself.

"There's nothing there," Alex said again. "Let's keep moving.

They continued walking to the end of the machine, but their hearing was focused. Every footstep and creak of metal seemed to echo ominously, resounding against their eardrums and competing with the sound of their heartbeat.

Alex examined the catwalk over the water. On the other side was another machine like this one. The island of metal was centered in a pool of light, cast by one of the few working overhead lights far above.

Gently at first, and then with more force, he kicked the walkway. "It seems to be safe. One person at a time."

He crossed gingerly. Once on the other side, he examined the path ahead. Nothing seemed out of the ordinary. "Come on. One at a time."

Quinn went next, gripping the hand-rails but moving faster than Alex had. Again, there was no indication the walkway was structurally compromised. Ryan was tempted to ignore Alex's direction and cross immediately, but common sense quelled that urge.

When Quinn made it to the other side unharmed, Ryan began his journey. He ignored the hand-rail and moved at a brisk walk. If he had followed Quinn's example, he might not have fallen backwards when the end behind him detached.

The sound of metal screeching filled the air, the echoes distorting into an eerie wail. Ryan had almost reached the end of the bridge, and when the walkway dropped from under him he flailed for the railings. He didn't find them where they were, but mercifully his outstretched arms managed to latch on before he tumbled into the water. Oil splashed his clothes.

Before he could right himself, an oily shape broke the disturbed surface. A tentacle dripping thick, black liquid raised high above them, and brought itself crashing down on the other end of the bridge as if trying to sever it completely.

Ryan hauled himself to his feet through sheer force of will. Alex and Quinn watched in shock as another tentacle snaked its way up the catwalk.

The thick tendril reached for Ryan's foot. With a force he didn't know he possessed, he stomped as hard as he could on the intruding appendage. The darkness was split with a deep rumble, seemingly more in challenge than pain.

Urged by adrenaline and panic, Ryan climbed to the upward end of the bridge. Alex and Quinn pulled him up and together they ran along the spine of the machine.

Their path was blocked by another pair of tentacles, lashing out from beyond the pool of light. The sickly green skin dripped with oil and oozed a foul-smelling ichor.

Ryan picked up a length of pipe and swung it like a club. Quinn tried a power tool before settling on a thin roller with a sharp, pointed end.

A blood-curdling scream came from behind them. They turned to see Alex being dragged backwards toward the collapsed bridge. Quinn rushed to help, but Ryan was attacked by the tentacles ahead of him.

They dove and stabbed, but Ryan managed to fend them off. Every attack was met with steel. But the impacts didn't seem to do any damage, and the tendrils continued their advance.

He looked back to see Quinn pulling Alex to relative safety near the center of the machine. A tentacle reached down from above, aiming for the pair. Ryan yelled a warning. Quinn looked at Ryan, not comprehending the danger, but before Ryan could explain he was hit from behind. Ryan stumbled, trying to catch his balance. The tentacle slapped him again, and he tumbled over the railing and into the inky black water.

Immediately he was swallowed by darkness. It had been dark before, but here there was no light whatsoever. His panic threatened to overwhelm him, but he stayed calm and tried to push off the floor. When he realized he couldn't touch the bottom, his panic returned with a vengeance. His eyes searched the complete darkness in vain. Every direction seemed to be down. Only when a beam of light pierced the oil above him did his panic subside. When he broke the surface, only a handful of seconds had passed. He gulped air as if he had been down for hours.

"Ryan!" Quinn called out from the walkway. Tentacles still circled him, but there seemed to be fewer. "There's a ladder over here!"

The direction Quinn pointed was blocked by a group of conveyor belts. They were too bulky to climb up on, and too long to go around. Ryan sucked in as much air as he could, and dove underneath.

This time, he was closer to the light from the overhead. The distant light dimly penetrated the layer of oil. The floor of the factory was black and slimy. It was littered with barrels, boxes, and debris fallen from the machinery above. Alex said it was only one meter deep, but it could have been anywhere from three to five meters.

He grabbed a bundle of cables floating in the current and pulled himself along. More shapes floated in the darkness, just out of his vision. When he peered closer, some of them became cables and wires and insulation. Others became tentacles jabbing at him.

Ryan swam faster. He twisted and kicked, and although none of the tentacles touched him, his attacks swept through empty water.

With a burst of effort, he cleared the conveyors above him and surfaced again. He scrambled up the ladder and looked around for the others. Alex was cowering in a hatch, but Quinn was surrounded in the open.

Ryan ducked as a tentacle swung at him. Quinn fell backwards, and something shiny fell out of his pocket.

Ryan tried to make his way to Quinn as the accountant picked up the object and looked at it intently. After a few seconds, he flicked the button and a tendril of fire flared up.

"Quinn, no!" Ryan shouted as Quinn picked up a rag and held it to the lighter. A tentacle almost struck Quinn, but retreated quickly when the cloth burst into flame. From deep beneath them, something screamed in anger and fear. The tentacles pulled away and bobbed in the darkness, as if afraid of accidentally igniting the lake of oil.

Bits of metal reflected the firelight as Quinn walked purposefully to the edge of the walkway. Ryan rushed Quinn and grabbed his wrist before he could drop the rag.

Quinn struggled a little and looked at Ryan. His eyes were bloodshot. "We have to burn it! We're dead if we don't!"

The heat from the fire scorched his hands. Ryan did his best to pull Quinn away from the edge. "If you light the oil, you'll incinerate us all!"

Quinn lunged and threw the fiery cloth over the railing. It fell slowly, twisting in the air until it draped itself over a pipe a meter above the water.

Ryan didn't have time for a sigh of relief. He felt a hand on his shoulder. It was Alex. "Run!"

The tentacles stayed at the edge of his vision, barely visible in the darkness. The trio blindly rushed for the exit, still a hundred meters away. Metal grating creaked and groaned, but it held.

Looking over his shoulder, he could still see the rag burning. A tiny candle in the darkness, threatening to ignite an inferno if it slipped.

Finally, they reached the end. The walkway led to a brightly lit corridor. They collapsed inside and caught their breath. Quinn looked shaken.

Outside, on the factory floor, it was silent. The tiny flame in the distance flickered and died. Ryan looked at Alex. "Is that one of your unexplainable phenomena?"

"No, actually, I can explain this one." Alex slowly stood and pulled out three disposable face masks. "Put these on."

Ryan pinched the metal band around his nose. "What is it?"

Their guide pointed to a yellowish slime oozing from between the wooden paneling. "Orange mold. I've never seen it this far out. The spores it releases cause hallucinations. Nothing you saw in there was real."

Ryan jumped to his feet. "You mean we weren't in any danger? That was terrifying!"

"No, we were definitely in danger. Everything we saw was a hallucination, but everything we did was real."

Quinn was mortified. "I tried to light the oil!"

Alex nodded. "Yes, we're lucky you didn't. Panic is common with these hallucinations. Some people end up stabbing things, or overdosing, or drowning, or immolating themselves."

"No, that was too real." Ryan sat back down, prodding the mask around his mouth. "Did we all hallucinate the same thing? Quinn, did you see how I went in the water?"

"Yeah, you swung at something, tripped, and fell over the railing."

"Huh. I thought it pushed me."

Alex straightened his hoodie. "Did you both see tentacles?"

"Yes," they answered.

"I saw vines. Some kind of plant monster. I think it was Ryan's comment about something green near the beginning. We all started to imagine a green monster, and the bridge collapse triggered the hallucinations."

Quinn looked at Ryan. "Was it just the tentacles, or the body too?"

"I might have seen the body underwater, but it was mostly just tentacles."

"For me, the squid climbed onto the machinery, blocking our path. It didn't leave until I lit the lighter."

Alex pulled the hood over his head. "You'll want to cover as much skin as possible. You can get a nasty rash."

"From mold?"

"It's called the Mold Swamp, but there's all kinds of fungi and algae, and other things that don't need natural light. Watch where you step, and don't touch anything."

With those instructions, they journeyed into the swamp.

The air was thick and humid. The ubiquitous wooden paneling drooped like wax, and the occasional carpet squelched like mud.

Ryan paused at a thick operator's manual left on a counter. Mushrooms sprouted from the pages like an illustration from a fairytale.

Lighting was erratic, but there was enough to see by. Ryan almost preferred the dark hallways because less flora grew there, but what did grow made him wish he could see better.

Rarely, flies or other insects would wander through the decaying ruin. Patches of moss were the only pleasant sight.

"I'm surprised this branch still has power." Ryan's voice was muffled from the spare jacket wrapped around his face.

"Me too, actually." Alex stepped around a package of rotting paper plates. "I don't know what electrical systems they installed, but easily ninety percent of the abandoned sections still have power. Even places that lost lighting only need more light bulbs."

Quinn coughed lightly. "Why aren't we using LEDs? Wouldn't those last longer?"

"Most of them are LEDs, but even those don't last forever. As the original ones burn out, the ones in paths are replaced. A couple years ago the Landonites uncovered a huge cache of lights, and through trading, they were spread throughout the non-loyalist territories. Areas like this are still lit because people pass through them. Although, it's not unusual to break open a secure area and find the lights still on from twenty years ago."

"I can't imagine the power bill this place has."

"There's a nuclear reactor powering just this building. You have to remember, though, most of the factories in the abandoned sections are shut down. The power cost is a lot lower now than when it opened."

Ryan and Quinn looked at Alex. "This place has a nuke plant?"

"Don't worry, it's still in loyalist hands and heavily regulated. They won't abandon that until they shut down for good."

They passed through a door with moss growing on the frame. The section beyond was a step lower, and a few centimeters of water covered the floor. Wooden boards made bridges over the murky pool.

Cables hanging from the walls intertwined with vines climbing from the floor. Piles of furniture hosted moss and fungus. Pale green plants sprouted from islands of mud. An occasional insect buzzed past their heads. The heavy, humid air was filled with the stench of decay.

But despite the smell, there was something beautiful about the place. Moss grew on the walls. Luminescent spores drifted on unseen air currents. The wild had reclaimed this portion of the factory, and a sunless forest was expanding through the concrete walls.

They rounded a corner to see a conference room. Tattered, mold stained projector screens hung like pirate flags against the dark green walls. The boardwalk ended at a stairwell on the other side of the hall.

"The mold swamp goes on a lot further on this level, but up above the walking is easier." Alex stepped from the boards to the bottom step. The water rippled as the soggy board flexed against its supports. "Once we're at the top, it's a straight shot to the Foundry Bay settlement."

Quinn adjusted the cloth over his face. "What's at Foundry Bay?"

"It's an independent community. They're not happy with the Tower, but they aren't rebelling either. They'd probably be loyalist if they could. But you can buy supplies and rest a while."

The swamp's influence waned on the higher levels, and after they passed through a sealed fire door it vanished completely. Like the rest of the factory, bland wallpaper and dirty floor tiles stretched as far as their flashlights could see along featureless hallways.

After a few more minutes, they reached the settlement. The main doors were a set of heavy fire doors that had been moved to standard door frames. Bare metal plates had been haphazardly welded over sections of rust.

"Hey! What business do you have here?" A guard, wearing a tattered blue cloak that seemed to pass for a uniform, warily glanced around the hall while keeping them in his sight.

Alex pulled his hoodie down. "I'm escorting employees from the Tower-"

"Alex! You're early! Did you bring the batteries we asked for?" The guard dropped all his wariness and stepped forward to greet the vending machine stocker.

"I'm afraid not, Matt. As I was saying, I'm not here in an official capacity. These poor men are from the Tower, and they got caught up in drama with the Landonites. I'm helping them escape."

"Oh, that's rough. Still, the Landonites have no influence this far out. Why did you bring them all the way here?"

"They're trying to get back to the Tower, Matt. Not relocate. Can you let us in?"

"Oh. Yeah, follow me." Matt sounded disappointed. He turned to Ryan and Quinn as he knocked on the fire door. "Why'd you want to live in some dingy old Tower, anyway? All the fun is down here!"

Ryan shrugged. "I like things like running water and internet. No offence."

"None taken. But we have all that too!"

Alex nodded. "They do. The infrastructure is intact enough that most wall jacks are still connected to the network. But just because there's running water, it doesn't mean anyone cleans the bathrooms."

Matt scoffed at Alex, but didn't reply. The door unlatched from the other side and swung open.

The main room of the Foundry Bay settlement was a former warehouse. Metal stairs and walkways were attached to the walls, leading to windows and doorways that didn't look standard. On closer inspection, it appeared holes had been cut in the warehouse walls into the adjoining rooms, and doors fabricated to fill them. They were joined by a metal balcony that Ryan guessed was built by the residents. The result was multiple levels of housing leading to a common area.

About twenty people looked at them as they walked in. Ryan was sure they didn't get many visitors. Most greeted Alex and he repeatedly apologized for not bringing goods. One of them seemed more official, and Alex introduced them.

"Richard, this is Ryan and Quinn. They're visiting from the Tower. Ryan and Quinn, this is Richard Herman. He's in charge of smithing, but he'll know how to help you." Richard was a balding man wearing a gray apron. A pattern of burn marks and acid splotches checkered the heavy cloth.

Richard shook their hands. "Please to meet you. Are you here on inspection?"

"No, we're just passing through. It's quite a lovely place you've built here."

"We did our best. Foundry Bay is the foundry for the old factory, and we have the best metal workers and tools."

Ryan looked around again. All the furniture was made of metal. "That's why it's called Foundry Bay?"

"Exactly. The Foundry itself is through those doors." Richard pointed to an open vehicle door at the far end of the warehouse. Beyond, rows of machinery sat idle. "This is a relatively safe place. We don't get many visitors, but the more violent parties are deterred by the swamp. On the other side, of course, we have the Frigid Wastes. No one knows what's in the Unknown Regions beyond that."

"Frigid Wastes?"

"Did Alex tell you where you're headed?"

Quinn shook his head. "We've been moving pretty quickly. I've barely had time to think about where I was, much less our destination."

Alex leaned in. "The Frigid Wastes is the informal name for sections 152 and 153. A few years ago, the temperature dropped almost instantly and a settlement there was abandoned. Most of the refugees joined Foundry Bay. As for the other side, the Unknown Regions, old assembly lines for the Model Twelve product line. There are rumors of a loyalist outpost somewhere but, as far as I know, no one has explored the wastes or beyond for years."

"And you're taking us there?"

"Actually, I'm not." Alex looked pained. "I'd love to, but my own experience ends at Foundry Bay, and I've neglected my supply routes for too long already. Acid Springs needs shoes and a ton of lime-flavored gummy worms. I'll find something to eat and be on my way. Richard can help you find a guide, but you should probably rest up and stay the night."

Richard nodded. "We'll be sorry to see you go, but we'll take good care of our guests."

Ryan cut in. "What about our destination?"

"The train station in section 152 should still be operational. Even if it isn't, the engineer's station should have a switch to contact dispatch and arrange extraction."

"Hold on." Quinn looked thoughtful. "If you have internet, can't we just contact someone that way?"

Alex and Richard looked at him. "Who would you contact?"

"...The factory foreman? The Tower? We have the helicopter pilot..."

"There's no way to the roof from here. And there's nothing anyone outside can do either." Richard put a hand on Quinn's shoulder. "If it was as simple as talking to the Tower, we'd tell them to get us out of here too."

At Richard's insistence, Alex, Ryan, and Quinn joined him and several others for dinner. After dessert, they said their goodbyes and Alex left Foundry Bay.

The guest rooms were clean and comfortable, although the furniture was outdated and worn. Most of the living quarters were the same as when the factory was first built. A digital TV hung on the wall, although the resolution was no longer capable of displaying modern television. It was only useful for the old-fashioned gaming console below it, probably used by the local children.

After a shower and a night's rest, they visited Richard again.

Richard looked apologetic. "I'm sorry to tell you this, but the best person to take you to the train station is also our best stamp operator. With the big order from Olan Depths due in a couple days, we can't spare him for a while. No one else is familiar with the area. You'll have to stay here a bit longer."

Ryan frowned. "Are you sure there's no other way?"

"I'm afraid not. We apologize for the inconvenience."

"We can't stay much longer. We've been gone too long already!"

"I still have the map on my tablet." Quinn turned it on and opened the map. "The station is marked on the map, and even if a path is blocked we can find a way around it."

The older man shook his head. "I don't recommend going by yourselves, even with a map. But if you do go, we have some warm clothing for sale."

"I don't think we have a choice. We need to get moving. But what currency do you use? We don't have any bottlecaps, or pre-war cash..."

Richard blinked. "We accept credit cards. The market has a point of sale machine."

Ryan looked embarrassed. "Oh. Right."

A few minutes later, Ryan and Quinn had eaten breakfast and donned some ill-fitting winter clothing. Tailoring was not Foundry Bay's strong suit, and the patched cloth was course and heavy. They both bought rechargeable flashlights, although they were expensive.

They left the main gate and journeyed deeper into the factory. Not many people had gone this way. A few parts had been scavenged, but the dust was thick and trash was absent. What debris there was came from lack of maintenance rather than vandals.

Quinn stopped in front of a hallway. They were standing in a warehouse. Shelves reached for the ceiling ten meters above, and cast eerie shadows in the dim light of their flashlights.

"What is it?" Ryan zipped up his coat. Chilled air flowed from the hallway and around his ankles.

"The second server room Fred marked. It's close." Quinn held his tablet so Ryan could see the map.

"Is it still worth trying to find it?"

"It's almost on the way. Looks like an hour detour. What do you think?"

Ryan thought for a moment, and nodded his head. "We may as well. I hope to never come this way again."

They moved into the hallway, and cold enveloped them.

Puddles of water dotted the floor. Unlike the swamp, there was no sign of life. Also unlike the swamp, they could see their breath. It was probably too cold to grow here.

"It should be right about..." Quinn turned a corner and pointed. "There. IR7152-31"

The light in the hallway still worked, although it only showed bare concrete walls. The server room door was half-hidden next to a metal tank in a recess.

A faded sign on the dark-blue door read "Authorized Personnel Only" in big letters. Other signs were too faded to read any more.

"Finally." Ryan inserted a key. "This door looks really heavy."

Quinn pointed to a red label. "It's a fire door. If there was a fire in this section, the equipment inside needs to stay safe."

The next key Ryan tried turned, but the door remained closed. "It's stuck." He pushed harder, but it only budged slightly."

"On three. One, two, three!" Both of them body slammed the door and it burst open. Ryan caught himself on the frame before he fell into the room.

The inside was dark, and quiet. Ryan took a step in and fumbled for the light switch. It didn't work. His hand came away black and gritty. Twisted server racks stood in rows. Cables hung between boxes and cable trays. Sheets of scorched plastic hung from bare copper wires as if melted and refrozen. Faint blue light from the room above filtered through cracks in the ceiling.

Quinn swept his flashlight across the grisly room. Everything was covered in soot.

Ryan covered his mouth with his sleeve. Their intrusion had raised a fine cloud of ash and he didn't want to breathe it. "A fire? How could this happen?"

"I don't know." Quinn's voice was muffled as he did the same. "Is there anything we can salvage? Maybe in the cabinets?"

A diagram or a map hung on the wall. Ryan tried to brush it off, but it crumbled on contact with his fingers. The cabinets held thick binders and manuals, but most were filled with ashes. One binder that seemed unscathed had laminated pages melted together.

The ever present cold made the scene even more surreal. Evidence of intense heat mixed with the dim blue light and goosebumps on their arms to produce a contradiction of the senses. Eventually they gave up.

"There's nothing here." Ryan stumbled into the hall, tracking ash on his shoes, and collapsed onto a short electrical cabinet. "How could there be a fire?"

Quinn leaned against the door frame. "At least the fire door worked. The fire was just on the wrong side."

Ryan chuckled and stood up. "I suppose we should keep going."

Their journey continued deeper into the wastes. The air grew colder. There were fewer puddles of water on the floor, and more patches of ice. Icicles hung from burst pipes. Frost glittered against the beams of their flashlights.

Sometimes a collapsed girder or a wall of ice blocked their path. Usually it was easy to get around. Sometimes the obstacles were man made. They were almost at the station when they found another one.

Quinn knelt on the floor to look at the door frame. His flashlight centered on the welds joining the frame and the door. "It's solid. Someone sealed this up."

"Can we go around?"

"I'll check." Quinn pulled up the map again and spent a few minutes reading.

While Quinn was busy, Ryan examined the door again. Other than being welded shut, it seemed perfectly normal. He wiped the dust off, looking for signs, and made a discovery. "Hey, this door has a window!"

Quinn stood up. "Can you see through it?"

"No, the other side must be dusty. I didn't even recognize it until I cleaned it. Hey, what if we..." Ryan hunted around the room until he found a metal rod. Before Quinn could stop him, Ryan smashed the glass.

"Hey!" The glass cracked, but did not shatter.

After a few more swings, Ryan gave up. "Must be reinforced."

"What are you trying to do? We can't fit through it anyway."

"I thought we might learn something useful. I don't know." Ryan dropped the rod and sat down on the concrete floor.

Quinn carefully put his hand on the cracked window. Threads of bitterly cold air squeezed through the cracks. He wasn't sure if it was his imagination or if Ryan's assault knocked some dust off, but a faint blue glow pulsed ominously on the other side. He took his hand away and pulled his coat tighter. "I don't like this. There might be a way around, but someone sealed this door to keep people out, or something in."

"What else can we do? Go back to Foundry Bay?" Ryan grabbed the tablet from where Quinn left it. "We could cut through the offices. Is that what you're thinking?"

"Yeah, but if we go up a level it might be easier. Plus, we might avoid whatever it is we're not supposed to find."

Ryan looked at the door again. "Some ancient evil, locked away in a freezing office building? Really?"

Quinn shrugged. "Or a gas leak, or fire hazard. There's enough danger in this factory without looking for more."

"Yeah, I guess."

They backtracked to a nearby stairwell and climbed up a level. Every surface was covered in frost, like the inside of a freezer. A cold breeze flowed past them in the icy tunnel. A few hundred meters from the station, a sound like a freight train reverberated through the floor. But unlike a train, it did not recede into the distance.

The station doors were buried in sheets of ice. Windows were frosted over. Vents and holes in the ceiling spewed frigid wind.

Ryan raised his voice above the noise. "I don't think we're going to find anything! Should we go in?"

Quinn didn't hear him. He was moving from window to window, tapping on the glass. "This one's loose! I think we can pry it free!"

Ryan knelt in the snow next to him. "There can't be anything here! If the inside looks anything like this, the train can't even get to us!"

"We have to try! Grab something to use as a lever!"

There wasn't anything nearby. The corridor was filled with five centimeters of snow and ice. Every wall had at least a centimeter of frost.

Ryan kicked at an electrical panel until a solid sheet of ice broke apart. He congratulated himself on his cleverness until he finally forced open the panel to reveal the insides covered in frost.

He turned back to Quinn, but the man wasn't at the window. Ryan started to panic until the beam of Quinn's flashlight came back down the hallway. He was carrying a fire axe.

Quinn stopped in front of the loose window. The first swing shattered the ice covering the glass. The second hit the center and a spider web of cracks appeared. He raised the axe a third time but, before he could swing, the cracks radiated across the window and the glass exploded outwards. Ryan barely had time to close his eyes before glass shards blew across his face.

The noise had been loud before, but now a hurricane roared through the hallway. Quinn fell over from the force of the wind. The air was filled with ice particles. The constant rush of air picked up any loose snow and blew it back the way they came.

Ryan tried to sit up. Quinn saw him and rushed over. He positioned his body to block most of the wind. "Ryan, you're bleeding! Don't move!"

At least his face was already numb. Quinn carefully removed the pieces of glass. The first aid kit in his backpack took care of most of the wounds, but Ryan was pretty sure his face would scar. Quinn's fingers were white with cold by the time he finished.

"Let's look at what we found!" Quinn pulled Ryan through the gap, fighting the icy wind. Ryan's breath froze in his nostrils.

The train station was full of odd shapes, none of them recognizable under layers of ice. The blizzard made it difficult to see more than ten meters. The particles of ice in the air scattered the light and reflected it back at them.

Unlike the normal frost, this ice had been blasted smooth from the gale still swirling through the station. It took a few minutes to realize what they were looking at.

A row of boxes two meters tall resembled a train on its side. The haphazard layout furthered that assumption. Piles and lumps scattered over the platform made no sense until he looked up and discovered sections of the ceiling had fallen away, leaving a large hole into the floor above. It was through this hole the wind originated.

Quinn was shouting something, but even half a meter away Ryan couldn't make it out. He pointed to a door on the side. Quinn took the axe and pounded on the door until the ice fell off.

Ryan pushed the door shut and collapsed against it. It didn't close all the way, but he leaned into it.

Quinn rubbed his fingers together. "I think I know what happened. The HVAC center, or something, is in the room above the station. A train derailed and somehow damaged the HVAC. Ever since, the air conditioning has been pushing out freezing air into this section. That might explain why the basement is hot and dry. This part of the HVAC is sucking up all the moisture and trapping it here."

"Do you really think so?"

"It's possible. It doesn't really matter. You're right, there's no way to get back to the Tower from here."

They sat in silence for a while, listening to the wind howl behind the door. "Do you think anyone was on the train?"

"I don't know. It could have been automated. Fatalities would have gathered a lot of attention, and I don't think anyone knows about this. Not even Foundry Bay knew."

"So now what? Do we go back to Foundry Bay? Live out the rest of our lives as metal workers?"

Quinn shrugged. "Maybe there's another way. There's roof access somewhere. It doesn't show it on my map, but if we look long enough we'll find it. There might be other ways out, too. We could follow the train tracks, or explore other sections."

"It could take months."

"Yeah, but we'll only have hours if we stay here. I can't feel my hands."

Ryan stood up. "First, we need to find a place with enough ventilation and fuel for a fire. Furniture or something. Then we can try to escape the Frigid Wastes and explore the Unknown Regions."

The semi-circular auditorium flickered with firelight. The glow from the flames illuminated the first few rows of stepped seating, a small island in the cold and darkness. The far walls and ceiling were beyond sight. If Ryan looked hard enough, he could see the reflection of the fire on the faux marble columns at the very back of the room.

Quinn shuffled from the sideroom to the podium where the fire was. He carried an armful of books. "I think these have been plastic treated. They're in better shape than I expected." He dumped the pile on the floor and tossed a book on the fire. "I'm sure this is a metaphor for something."

"Burning books to stay alive? It does carry a certain despair. What are we burning anyway?"

The accountant grabbed a book and read the title. "Super-Dynamic Fluid Analysis for Dummies."

"Nothing terribly important, then." Ryan leaned back from the heat. "Are you ready to eat?"

"Yeah."

Ryan opened his backpack and pulled out two plastic-wrapped sub sandwiches they bought in Foundry Bay. "I think we have enough food for another day, unless we happen across another vending machine. After that, we'll need to return to Foundry Bay."

"As long as the food is non-perishable. Nothing out here has been restocked for years." Quinn tossed the wrapper on the floor. "I hate to litter, but it's not as it there's a trashcan nearby."

Ryan, chewing on his own sandwich, turned and pointed to a half-full bin lying on its side.

"Very funny. We also need to watch the batteries in the flashlights."

"Let's try to use one at a time. And we might not need light while we're resting."

"Good idea." Quinn swallowed. "And I still have my lighter. I wonder if we could make a torch?"

The rest of their meal continued in silence. Afterward, they stomped out the fire and walked on.

The air was still cold, but it grew warmer the further they traveled from the damaged train station. When the patches of ice became puddles again, Ryan allowed himself to celebrate. But their objective was still out of reach.

Even though they had effectively given up on finding the desk phone to gain access to the sales database, Quinn tried to guide them to the third server room anyway. There was no other goal on this side of the wastes, and Ryan preferred it to wandering aimlessly. But the Unknown Regions were confusing.

They found several rooms and intersections that shouldn't exist. Before long, Quinn had to admit they were lost.

Backtracking was only partially successful. They found themselves in a completely different section and had somehow gone down a level, despite not using any stairs. Further on, the wall markers were missing and any indications of their position was gone.

Ryan sat on a conference room chair that had been left in the hallway. "I don't get it. Why take the room numbers? Nothing else is missing."

Quinn was busy with the map, as usual. "Turn the flashlight off. We need to conserve power."

The flashlight went off and the only light came from the screen of Quinn's tablet. Ryan watched over his shoulder as he tried to compare the layout from memory.

"Did you hear that?" Ryan flicked the flashlight on and swept it up and down the hall.

Quinn looked up and listened for a few seconds. "No, I don't hear anything." He continued studying the map.

Ryan tried the nearby doors, but they were all locked. He rejoined Quinn and switched the flashlight off again. "Have you found anything?"

"I'm pretty sure we're here, on level seven. Therefore, we need to go that way." He pointed down the hall into the dark.

Quinn turned off the tablet and reached for his own flashlight. For a second, they were in total darkness.

Something felt wrong. The darkness was almost tangible. He was aware of every centimeter of his skin exposed to the cool air. In his confusion, he fumbled with the switch on the flashlight. It was another second of panic before he finally got the light on and swept it around. Nothing threatening appeared, but Ryan looked just as terrified as he was.

"Did you feel that?"

Ryan nodded.

"Let's keep moving, but stay close. Keep at least one light on at all times."

Ten minutes later, Quinn was staring at the map in confusion again.

"It doesn't make sense! If we aren't on level seven...maybe three? No, that's not possible. Ryan, was it a hundred meters from the last intersection, or a hundred twenty?"

Ryan was examining rust stalactites hanging from a cluster of pipes. "I...don't know."

"What are you looking at?"

The salesman put his hand on the leaky pipe. "There's water moving through here."

"Of all our concerns, I don't think a water pipe is very high. Now, where..." He trailed off as a low grinding noise resonated from deep below them.

Ryan and Quinn looked at each other. The sound came twice more and stopped.

Quinn pointed at the pipes. One end came up from the floor. The other followed the corridor into the distance. "Let's follow the water. It might lead to something interesting."

Two more bursts of sound echoed through the empty halls. One was a shrill, mechanical screech. It almost seemed to come from next door, but a brief search found nothing that could have caused it. Half an hour later, the second was so low and distant they felt more than heard it.

Ancient machines, misfiring and malfunctioning. Most of the power was dead. But some circuits were still live, Ryan reasoned, so it would make sense for electrical shorts to activate parts of the machinery that surrounded them in every direction. Quinn wasn't as sure. Ryan insisted he sells electrical equipment and was the expert this time.

Finally, they stopped in a foyer. Small metal archways were connected with chains to mark paths through the room. Bulky, dust covered boxes and conveyor belts were haphazardly pushed to the side. It looked oddly familiar, as if he should recognize it, but the monochrome layer of dust made it difficult to guess. Several signs covered the walls. Quinn wiped one off. It said "No recording devices allowed".

Beyond that was a set of heavy blast doors. One was open just enough to squeeze through. The passage beyond looked the same but, a hundred meters later, it opened into a massive cavern.

Ryan and Quinn swept their flashlights up and down the structure. A circular shaft, ten meters wide, extended far above and below them. Objects like giant internal gears surrounded the hole on circular tracks every ten meters down. Other things, robotic arms and rods and spikes, extended into the space. Wire troughs carried pipes and cables in every direction. Around the sides, crates and tool carts interspersed piles of equipment they couldn't identify.

They took a few moments to absorb the sight. "I've never heard of anything like this," Quinn said.

"Is it on the map? Maybe we can figure out where we are."

Quinn didn't take his eyes off the imposing structure. "No, it's not."

"Look, stairs." Ryan pointed to a stairwell connecting the levels. "Although it's a bit..."

Quinn examined the twisted metal that had once been a set of steps. The concrete floor was cracked, and a nearby mass of machinery had also been demolished. "We can't go up."

"Down doesn't look promising either." The stairs above had been compacted into a tangle of railing and supports.

Quinn pointed to a large number painted on the wall. "At least we know we're on level six. Too bad we can't get down to four."

Their footsteps echoed faintly as they walked around, looking for anything that might be useful. Ryan studied a four meter long robotic arm, and noticed hand holds on the sides. "Hey. maybe we could climb this thing."

The arm ended in open space over the hole, near a cluster of pipes. The pipes ran at an angle to reach a walkway on the fifth level. Quinn looked at it dubiously. "It's a long way down if we fall."

"Should we stay up here and look around more?"

"Yeah. There might be another way down, or even something we can use to escape."

But after an hour of searching the surrounding rooms, they didn't find anything except towers of machinery. They returned to the hole.

"I really don't like the look of this," Quinn said. "I vote we move on."

Ryan shook his head. "I say we try it. We can't just wander around and hope to find something. At least level four might get us closer to a working data communication center."

Quinn thought about it. "Alright. But be careful." The words "WEIGHT LIMIT 10000 KG" were painted on the side. He tested his weight on the robotic arm. It didn't budge.

The first section of the arm was tricky to climb, because it was parallel to the floor and two meters above it. Quinn had to step on the railing and straddled the arm, pulling himself along with the handholds. A meter out over the hole, an elbow joint pointed downward and to the left to the pipes.

Crawling backwards down the arm, Quinn paused at the elbow and gazed downward. Despite his focus on not falling, he absently noted that the center of the hole was clear all the way down. The various equipment was hugging the sides.

Ryan held the flashlight steady as Quinn passed the elbow. But his path took him under the lip of the concrete platform.

Quinn stopped and considered his options. "I'll stop here for now." He carefully reached into his pocket and withdrew his own flashlight. "I'll cover you while you come down."

"Can you hang on and use the flashlight at the same time?"

"I'm not going anywhere. As long as only one of us is moving, and the other holds a light, it should be fine."

"Alright, if you say so." Ryan's voice seemed a bit shaky.

"You aren't flaking out on me, are you? You wanted to climb down this way, and I'm already hanging over empty air."

Ryan secured his flashlight in his pocket and looked back at Quinn. "No, I'm fine", he said, in a tone that suggested this was the last thing he wanted to do. But despite his hesitation, he clambered up on the arm and made his way down. Quinn felt the metal jostle slightly, but there was no threat of collapse.

The salesman slowly descended to within a meter of Quinn and locked his legs around the arm. "I'll hold the flashlight while you get to the pipes. Ready?"

"Ready." Quinn's hands were getting slippery from sweat. He almost fumbled getting his flashlight back into his pocket, but he managed it. The arm ended in two meters, but there was a meter gap between the robotic grasper and the pipes. He kept three-point contact at all times as he climbed down. At the end of the arm, he carefully swiveled around so he was facing the pipes. He nervously glanced down. A single cable, three meters away, was the only lifeline if he fell. Below that, only empty darkness waited.

With a strength that surprised himself, he jumped from the arm and landed precariously on the pipes. He immediately wrapped his arms and then his legs, hanging on for his life.

"Are you good?"

Quinn waited a second for his heart rate to calm down. "I'm fine." He tested his weight on the pipes. Completely solid. It helped that the supports were bolted to the wall every few meters. He crawled further down to make room for Ryan. "I'll hold the flashlight now."

"Okay." Ryan turned his flashlight off after Quinn activated his, and tried to insert it into his pocket.

From somewhere deep below, a grinding noise reverberated through the shaft. Quinn took his flashlight beam off Ryan for a second to look down, but only the same twisted shapes stood out.

"Hey," Ryan protested, "I can't see!"

"Sorry!" Quinn returned the beam to Ryan. A second noise filled the huge space. "I think you should hurry."

"I know! I can't get the flashlight in my pocket!"

Quinn suddenly realized the pipes were vibrating. It was so slight he didn't notice it at first, but it was building. With it came a gentle hum from all around them. "Hurry!"

Ryan finally began climbing down. He was almost halfway.

All at once, the shaft was filled with blinding light. Every overhead light came on, while dozens of smaller lights on the machinery began flickering.

Quinn's eyes adjusted, and he looked around frantically. Above them, maybe fifty meters, was a giant assembly in the center of the shaft. In the center of that was a glassy lens. Below was the same machinery he had seen earlier, but he also saw bands of copper wiring around the shaft between them and level five. It almost looked like a giant inductor.

The vibrations increased pitch sharply.

Movement at the bottom of the shaft caught his eye. One by one, the internal gear things slowly started spinning. The hair on his arms stood straight.

Ryan was at the end of the arm, but he was gripping the metal with all his strength.

Quinn grabbed a support beam with one hand and reached for Ryan with the other. He couldn't quite reach. "Give me your hand!"

The salesman looked absolutely terrified, but he cautiously loosened his grip. Just then, the gear assembly above them activated. With it, all manner of machinery woke around the shaft. The robotic arm Ryan still clung to swung to a position programmed into it decades ago. Ryan fell away and landed three meters below on a boxy protrusion. The flashlight burst from his pocket. It bounced off another robotic arm and tumbled down the shaft.

Quinn hesitated. Ryan seemed safe for the moment, but he could be hurt. There wasn't any way to get to him. Maybe if Quinn got to level five, he could find something to rescue Ryan.

Before he could take action, the cacophony of grinding and clanking was pierced with metal tearing. A machine above him was torn loose and fell in a tangle of debris and cables. Quinn held onto the supports as the machine smashed into the pipes next to him and continued down the shaft.

His path down to level five was demolished. The supports he clung to felt loose, and he wanted to move as soon as possible. He looked around for another option and saw the hanging cables from the fallen machine. Two more cables were hanging loosely halfway around the shaft, toward Ryan.

Quinn spent a moment calculating distance. He grabbed a cable and tugged. He almost stumbled when it came loose and fell. Only his flailing grip on the pipe supports saved him. He watched the cable snake through the air and wrap around a pylon twenty meters down.

Cautiously, he reached for another cable and tugged. When it held, he pulled with all his weight. It was firm.

Quinn wrapped his arms around the cable and jumped away from the wall, in the opposite direction of Ryan. He only traveled a few meters, but at the height of his swing he pushed off the wall again and swung toward the second group of cables. He desperately hoped they would hold as he let go of the first cable and grabbed a second.

His grip slipped and he fell a meter. His hands burned with friction. But he held on, and ran against the wall to maintain his momentum. He pushed off the wall a third time, and arced through the empty space of the shaft toward Ryan.

The trip unintentionally took him close to the center of the shaft. He suddenly felt heat on his face and hands, as if he were standing next to a furnace. He was through it just as suddenly, and Ryan was below him. Quinn loosened his grip and slid down the cable, landing roughly on the box Ryan was lying on. He accidentally kicked Ryan in the process, and both Ryan and Quinn would have slid off if Quinn hadn't grabbed Ryan with his left arm, the cable with his right, and the box itself with his legs. Ryan held on to Quinn for dear life.

They stayed like that for several seconds until Quinn was certain they weren't going to fall.

Still with a death grip on Ryan's shoulder, he turned to look at his buddy. "Are you okay?"

"My hip hurts where I landed, and my leg from where you hit me. I can't believe you did that!"

"Sorry. I didn't mean to."

"Not that. The swinging on the ropes! That was insane!"

"Yeah, but we're not done yet." Quinn tugged on the cable again. "This is our ticket out of here."

Ryan grimaced. "I can't do that. I think I strained something in my leg."

"It's okay. I'll climb down to level five while you hold the cable and keep me from swinging back into the shaft. Once I find something to secure it to, you can slide down and I'll catch you. Can you do that?"

"Yes, I'll try."

"Alright. Let's go." Without standing up, they shifted position on the box so the cable was resting on the rear, wedged against the support column. Quinn swung his legs over the side and carefully lowered himself the three meters to level five. His arms were already aching, and for a heartbeat he was sure he would lose his grip. But he made it down and collapsed on the hard concrete floor.

The whining noise increased pitch. The air shimmered, as if looking through a mirage. A column in the center of the shaft became nearly opaque with energy. Ryan slid down the cable and rolled onto the floor.

Lights flickered and failed. Sparks burst from transformers. All around them the hum of electricity reached a crescendo. The column of energy glowed a dull white.

All at once, everything shut off. The shaft was plunged into darkness. The whine of motors fell to silence.

Quinn pulled out his flashlight and examined the walls. The afterimage of the column was burned into his retinas.

"What now?" Ryan asked.

"I'm looking for radiation warnings or symbols. Something to explain what that thing was."

"Why?"

"I got pretty close to the beam. If it was powered by radiation, I won't live much longer. But I don't see anything."

Ryan looked concerned, but shrugged. "At least we can take the stairs to level four. Let's rest here before we go on."

Only Quinn had a flashlight now. Ryan stayed close behind. This section of the factory had an apocalyptic feel to it. It was as if the workers had dropped everything and walked away, and looters later returned to trash the rooms and pick through the goods. Books, tools, even pictures were scattered across the floor. But the looters themselves were long gone. All that remained was debris, trash, and broken machinery.

They found a cafeteria, but found it exactly as they expected. Not a speck of food remained. The vending machines were broken and tipped over, their empty carcasses sprawling around the room. Water still came from the faucet, but it was dark yellow.

They stopped in an access shaft to refill their canteens from the water mains running through the factory. In the light of a single flashlight, they continued through the unknown regions.

"What do you suppose that shaft was?" Quinn wondered aloud.

"If it wasn't on the maps, it must have been secret. I think the place in front of the doors was a security station."

"Of course! Those arches in the middle of the room were metal detectors, or body scanners. We passed another set when we left. As for the blast doors themselves, they were pretty heavy. We wouldn't have been able to move them ourselves. But were they protecting the shaft, or the rest of the factory?"

Ryan shrugged. "Maybe both? Are you thinking there was some risk from what they were building?"

"I'm just wondering. It must have been a huge secret to go as far as altering the maps."

"While we're on this, why did it wake up right then? It must have been abandoned for decades." Ryan kicked a chunk of concrete lying in the path. "Not only does everything still work, but it chose that exact moment to try to kill us?"

"I don't know," Quinn said thoughtfully.

"Thanks for saving me, by the way." Ryan turned to face Quinn. "I would have frozen up and gotten us both killed."

"Don't mention it. You saved us at the flooded factory. I would have burned us all if you hadn't stopped me. How's the hip, by the way?"

"I limp sometimes, but I don't think it's that bad."

"Let me know whenever you need to rest."

They walked in silence for a while.

Ryan kicked a wooden pole lying in the dust. The end of it hit the wall with a metallic clank. He stooped to pick it up, and Quinn's flashlight reflected off a metal spike strapped to the end.

"A spear?" Quinn bent closer. The metal attachment was a crude blade bound to the pole. It certainly appeared to be a weapon.

"Alex said none of the factions use weapons. Who does this belong to?"

"We're pretty far from faction territory."

Ryan dropped the spear back in the dust. "I don't like this."

Quinn swept the flashlight around before continuing down the hall. "Does that imply there was a part you did like?"

"The helicopter ride was pretty sweet."

"Yeah, it was. We should have stayed up there and talked to the pilot all day. I bet what he knows is more valuable than a twenty-year old database."

"Yeah."

The beam of the flashlight caught another glint. Another weapon lay half buried in rubble.

Quinn examined it. "It's almost exactly like the other one. I bet they used machinery to stamp out the blades. Maybe the poles, too."

"So these aren't two people with a disagreement. Someone was mass producing weapons for a conflict."

"Yeah. These aren't spears, though. This looks more like a glaive. Spears only have a point and are designed to thrust. This also has an edge for slashing, to make it easier to use without training."

Ryan looked amused. "How do you know this stuff?"

"Lots of Blood War 2. I hate to think about what else is down here." Just as he said that, they rounded a corner into a two-story chamber. It was about ten meters wide and forty meters long.

Old planters and overturned benches speckled the floor, but the dominating feature was a barricade. It was two meters tall, of furniture and debris. More spears, or glaives, stuck out of the barricade to discourage climbing.

They cautiously walked through the gap in the center, dreading what they would find but driven by morbid curiosity. To their relief, no bodies were visible anywhere.

Quinn picked up another weapon. "This one is different. The handle is longer. The blade is longer, too. Whoever designed this was afraid, and wanted to keep the enemy further away. But it's only useful out here in the open. In the corridors, the shorter version would have the advantage."

Ryan raised a hand. "Could you pause the forensics? People could have died here."

The accountant sighed. "Is it more respectful to figure out what happened, or ignore their deaths?"

"I...when you put it that way...could you be less smug about it?"

"Yeah. I'll try to be respectful. To be honest, there's not much more I can tell."

"Who won?"

"The lack of bodies is a good sign, but it makes it difficult to tell. This gap in the barricade doesn't look intentional, though. It would be difficult to defend." Quinn examined the debris outside the barricade. "It looks like it was torn apart from outside."

"So the defenders lost."

"Quinn thought out loud. "I wonder why the factions won't use weapons. It's not some philosophical enlightenment that they're above violence. They hate each other. They must feel the compulsion to build something, anything, that will give them an advantage."

"They've seen it before," Ryan finished Quinn's thought. "They know what happens when two sides try to kill each other."

"Now that I think about it, there is some good news. Not only are there no bodies, but none of these weapons have blood on them. There are no signs of struggle other than the barricade. They certainly came close to murdering each other, but there's no indication they did."

Ryan looked around. The battlefield was strewn with shadows, and he didn't want to look too hard at any of them. "Should we keep looking for clues?"

Quinn shook his head. "No, there could be anything in these rooms. Just because we haven't found any remains doesn't mean there isn't a pile of corpses somewhere. There could be things even worse, like traps or poison. Someone will learn what happened here, but it should be a full corporate security investigation. Right now, we owe it to them to get out alive and make a report."

"Yeah. This place gives me the creeps."

"Let's start working on the 'getting out alive' bit."

Ryan took a step and half collapsed against the wall. Quinn helped him up. "My leg is bothering me. I think I'll be fine after a rest. But not here. Let's get someplace less depressing."

They turned and left.

Quinn and Ryan were in a service hallway, one of hundreds that ran through the belly of the factory. The gray concrete and pipes made for hours of monotonous walking.

Ryan wished they were back in the rubble strewn halls and manufacturing floors. At least there were bits of color scattered through the debris. Faded paint, coded wires, even scraps of papers and magazines. Every single surface was either black or gray here. They could have gone colorblind and not even know it.

They tried a hatch which should have led into food processing, but found it was barred from the other side. Another hatch seemed to be jammed, but on closer inspection was welded shut.

Spider webs draped across the walkway clung to their clothing as they trudged on. Sometimes, the sound of dripping water echoed maddeningly through the concrete tunnel. They never found the sources.

Finally, they found an exit. The section they found themselves in had been painted in cheerful colors, but faded to almost monochrome. There was less trash here. Office furniture and vending machines stood intact, but empty.

Ryan tried not to think about their destination. They still had plenty of food from Foundry Bay. As long as they stayed close to the maintenance and service tunnels, they had as much water and electricity as they needed. But it started to look like they would be down here for a very long time. It was made worse that they needed to stop and rest often for his leg.

Quinn walked stoically, as if he knew exactly what he was looking for. But when they stopped and rested, Ryan could see his frustration as he fruitlessly studied the map.

Ryan had gotten in the habit of holding on to Quinn's shoulder with one hand. Quinn was the only one with a flashlight, and if Ryan somehow took a wrong turn he would be in total darkness. Even when they stopped, they maintained a grip on each other's arms, just for assurance of their presence.

They had been walking for hours. Ryan was looking to the side, trying to see into the rooms they passed. Quinn stopped walking, and Ryan bumped into him.

"What's wrong?"

"The flashlight is dim."

He was right. Usually the beam reached twelve meters ahead of them, but now they could barely make out details three meters away.

"Didn't you charge it the last time we stopped?"

"Yes!" The flashlight continued to fade. Darkness closed in around them.

"The tablet! Use the tablet!"

Quinn was already reaching into his pack. He withdrew the tablet and pushed the power button frantically. "I don't understand! This should be at full power!"

They looked at each other in the dying light, panic welling in their faces. At the last moment, just before the flashlight died completely, Quinn remembered his lighter.

The little flame did not light much, maybe a meter in each direction. They carefully shuffled forward. Walls were barely visible. Open doorways were gaping voids of blackness.

Only a few meters later, they reached an intersection. They stood in the center, gazing into the eternal night. The corners of the walls held no clues of their location.

Minutes passed. They stood still in the flickering light, the edges of the darkness only a meter away. A gust of wind, or a single breath, and it would rush in and claim them.

Ryan looked down one passageway, and then another. There was nothing there. Nothing in all this factory, but he kept straining his eyes in search of something, anything.

A sudden movement in the darkness grabbed his attention. He tensed up with fear as a shape formed, and suddenly he recognized it as Alex the vending machine supplier.

Ryan relaxed. "Oh, it's you! What are you doing here?"

Alex smiled and pulled off his signature hoodie. "I thought you could use some help. Come on. The exit is this way." Alex pointed down a hallway and turned, expecting them to follow.

"Ryan?" Quinn asked softly. "Who are you talking to?"

"What?" Ryan turned to Quinn. "It's Alex." He lifted his finger to point. "He's right—"

The hallway was empty.

Ryan jumped. He frantically turned and looked in every direction, but Alex was nowhere to be found. Only the two of them. He was close to hyperventilating.

Quinn grabbed him in a half hug, as if he expected Ryan to bolt from his grasp. The other hand held the lighter. "You're okay! You're okay! Calm down. What did you see?"

Ryan finally caught his breath. "It was Alex. He said he was here to show us the exit."

"And he just...showed up?"

"Didn't even have a light. He materialized out of the dark."

"Okay. Okay. What else?"

"Ummm...he pointed down one of the halls. Then I looked away, and he was gone."

Quinn loosened his grip. "Which way?"

Ryan had gotten turned around. He examined the tunnels again. "This way. No...this way."

"Are you sure?"

"Yes. It's definitely this one."

"It doesn't matter anyway. Let's try it. It has to be better than standing here."

Slowly, they crept forward into the tunnel. Nothing jumped out at them. No more visions appeared to Ryan. But after some time, they stopped and listened.

"I hear music," Ryan said.

"Are you sure it isn't a hallucination?"

But they listened some more, and finally Quinn heard it too. Cautiously, they inched closer to the sound.

They could almost make out the notes. "Classical, maybe?"

"Maybe. Could be Jazz."

They listened some more, trying to judge its direction.

Quinn inhaled sharply, and then breathed a sigh of relief. Ryan watched his face quizzically as the accountant stared into the inky darkness. "It's just you. Where did you go, Ryan?"

Ryan grabbed Quinn and spun him around. "It's not real! I'm right here!"

As soon as Quinn saw Ryan, he panicked and tried to get away. They wrestled for a moment, and Ryan was certain the lighter in Quinn's hand would go out. But Quinn relaxed, and went limp in his arms. They both sank to their knees, still holding each other.

Quinn's breathing slowly returned to normal. "So that's what you saw, Ryan? It was so real. I didn't even question it until I saw you next to me."

"What was it?"

"I saw you. Down to the last detail. Just walking into the light as if you had gone for a quick stroll."

"Did it say anything?"

"No. He looked like he was about to. What if you hadn't grabbed me, Ryan? I could have followed him somewhere without even thinking about it."

"It's okay. Everything will be okay." Ryan wished he could believe it.

Quinn's deep breathing continued. Ryan almost thought Quinn had fallen asleep in his embrace. But Quinn stood up after a few minutes. "I'm okay now. Sorry about that."

"That's fine. That's why I'm here."

"It's just, when you turned me around, I thought you were the vision. I thought you were going to abduct me, or something. And when I couldn't find your ghost, I thought you had abandoned me."

"It's okay. I'll never abandon you." This time, Ryan didn't have trouble believing that.

Quinn smiled. "I won't abandon you, either. You have my word."

"Now, about that music. Another hallucination?"

"I don't think so. None of our hallucinations were shared, even at the flooded factory. On the count of three, we'll both point in the direction we think it's coming from. One, two, three."

Both fingers pointed to another hall. The music steadily grew louder.

"It's definitely classical. Mozart?"

Quinn shrugged. "I wouldn't know. I was more interested in power metal in college."

The music got abruptly louder. They rounded a corner. Ryan noticed movement out of the corner of his eye. As he turned to look, a brilliant light filled the hallway.

Two figures stood in front of them. One was holding a flashlight. A bare light bulb on the wall behind them gave them a partial silhouette.

"Now there's two of them," one said.

"I see them too! What's going on?"

Ryan overcame his shock and tried to speak. "Umm, hello?"

They ignored him. "Have you tried closing your eyes?"

"Of course. They're still there."

Quinn still held the lighter. He wasn't sure what was going on, but it was probably another hallucination.

Ryan took a step closer. "Are you real?"

They finally turned to him. "We should be asking you that," the one with the flashlight said. "What do you want?" He took a mobile device out of his pocket and pushed a button. The music stopped.

"Umm..."

"What are your names?"

"I'm Ryan, and this is Quinn."

The one with the flashlight turned it off and motioned them into the light. "I'm Nathan. This is Pete. What are you doing here?"

"We were lost, and the power in our flashlight died-"

"Yeah, that happens." Pete interrupted Quinn. He motioned to the wall light. "Power's back on now."

Quinn tried his own flashlight. It worked. "What are you doing here?"

Nathan waved them forward. "I'll take you to our camp. It isn't far." He activated his light and walked. Ryan and Quinn followed cautiously, with Pete taking up the rear.

Cold white light spilled around the corner ahead of them. The light was mounted about a heavy steel hatch set into the concrete. Footprints in the dust led in every direction, and the handles on the hatch were shiny from use.

There was no way to open the hatch from outside. Nathan banged three times. Clicking and whirring noises came from inside, and the hatch slowly swung open.

Two more people, dressed in the tan-and-blue Tower uniforms stood in the room beyond. They all carried flashlights. They stared as Ryan and Quinn entered.

Finally one of the employees spoke. "Do I know you?"

Ryan shook his head. "I don't think so. Do we know you?"

"Sorry, the hallucinations can be tricky. In fact, I'm still not sure you're real." Nathan slammed the hatch shut and spun the handle to lock it. In the light, they got a better look at him. Like the others, he wore a blue and tan uniform. He was about their age, with a mop of clean but unruly brown hair. Pete had graying hair and a beard.

Quinn shrugged. "Same. Who are you?"

None of the uniforms had badges. The others introduced themselves.

"Blake." A young man with short cropped brown hair.

"Call me Donovan." The last employee cheerfully added. He was a bit older, with a heavy frame.

"I'm Ryan, and this is Quinn. We're from the Tower. What are you doing here?"

Nathan held up a hand and turned to the other three. "Does everyone else see them? What are their names?"

"Ryan and Quinn", they said in unison.

"And Samantha." Blake added.

Everyone turned to look at Blake.

"What? Are there only two of them?"

"Look again, Blake."

The young man blinked and looked past Ryan. "Drat. I was really hoping she was real. She was making eyes at me, too. I suppose the swimsuit should have been a give-away."

Nathan turned back to Ryan. "Are you here on an inspection? You don't look good."

Ryan and Quinn's clothes were covered in cobwebs and dust. "No, we were looking for something but got lost. Our map wasn't accurate."

Pete looked at them with suspicion. "Hold on. No one ever comes here except on purpose. Where did you come from?"

"Foundry Bay. We're originally from the Tower, but we got sidetracked."

"Foundry Bay? Where is that?"

"It's on the other side of the Frigid Wastes," Ryan said hesitantly. "You might have a different name for it. There's a broken AC unit a few kilometers west of here, and most of that section is frozen. Do you know what I'm talking about?"

Nathan shook his head. "We don't explore much. Certainly not that far away. You walked from there?"

Quinn laughed. "That was just today. We've been moving since yesterday. Why are you here?"

"We're maintaining critical assets for the Tower. Generators, and computers, and the like."

"You're in contact with the Tower?"

"Of course. We maintain a microwave network connection."

Quinn turned to Ryan. "This is the loyalist outpost!"

"Loyalist?"

"Those still in contact with management in the Tower. A lot of people down here aren't, whether by accident or choice."

Donavan stood up. "Let's discuss this over dinner. We've plenty of rations for two more. Then you can tell us your story."

The six of them sat down to eat. It was all pre-packaged meals, but much better than vending machine food. Ryan and Quinn took turns recalling the events since the helicopter ride. They left out some important details, like the search for the server rooms and purpose of their visit.

When they finished, Nathan put down his fork. "I knew parts of the factory were empty, but I had no idea it was that bad."

"It almost makes this section seem nice," Pete added.

Quinn interrupted. "Are hallucinations that big of a problem down here?"

Nathan shrugged. "Once or twice a month. We always go in groups of two, so if someone is affected the other can snap him out of it. The apparitions disappear as soon as you look away, and no one else can see them. But no matter how paranoid you are, you take it for granted that someone you know is wandering down here. Always someone from memory."

"Are they hostile? What do they want?"

"They try to lead you somewhere. I don't know if it's the same or a different place for each one. Even if you tried to follow them all the way, you would have to blink eventually and they're gone."

"My first time, I followed one for five minutes." Donavan leaned forward to tell his tale. "I was terribly confused when the illusion broke. The interesting thing is, I was an hour's walk from base. I'd be dead if I didn't have the map. They seem to lead you through portals or somethin.'"

"Actually," Nathan said, "A simpler explanation is that the victim loses track of time, or memory is affected after the event, or something similar. Portals are a bit of a stretch when we already have documented mental disruption."

"I'll admit, I forgot to check the time when I first saw it. But Blake can testify I was only gone for an hour and a half!"

"Yes, that is suspicious. But the only way to tell for sure is to grab a pocket watch and ask the nearest apparition for directions. I'll just as soon avoid that."

"What do you think causes them?" Ryan asked.

The four employees looked at each other.

"There's a lot that goes on down here," Nathan said. "The apparitions are one of the nicer events. We don't understand any of it."

"What did we agree on, again?" Pete asked.

"I don't recall agreeing to nothin'," Donavan said.

"The most commonly accepted theory," Nathan said, "Meaning Pete and I agreed, is that a secret government experiment irradiated this section with mind-altering X-rays."

"Hold on," Quinn interrupted. "First of all, X-rays can't alter minds. Except by microwaving them. And what else happens down here?"

"There's all sorts of phenomena that are beyond science. The apparitions are the most disturbing, but they're also rare and easily handled as long as you have a buddy nearby. Others are...less easily dismissed. There are sounds from deep below us. Sometimes even tremors. The factory power in these sections has been disconnected for years, but sometimes every electrical device will come back to life for a few minutes."

Ryan nodded. "Like in the shaft."

"But worst of all are the ones that happen in your mind. The apparitions are one, but the wires in your brain can get crossed. Your day will be happening as normal, and then you reach for something with your right hand and your left will move instead. You lose all muscle coordination for a few hours, and when you finally switch back you have to learn to walk again because your brain has already started to get used to the reversed inputs."

"It's still better than the organic brownouts. It's like your entire brain slows down, and you can feel your consciousness failing. It only lasts a few minutes, but it's absolutely terrifying."

"Twice in the last four years, I've woken up thinking it's the day after. You already remember every detail of every action you take that day, before you've even done them. Not déjà vu, either. Every single detail."

"What if you refused to follow your memory?"

Pete shook his head. "It's happened to me too, and the memories are never outlandish or unreasonable. It's always your normal daily routine, you just have the memories in advance. Those days, you just follow along in a kind of stupor. Like following a script."

"What else?"

"Sometimes...in the lower levels..." Blake started but paused, looking around as if asking for permission. They all looked non-committal. He continued. "Sometimes, you can hear voices. Never the words. Only the voices."

Nathan shrugged, but Pete added to it. "I've heard them too. As if from a distance. The first time, you can convince yourself it's just the echoes of footsteps, or water dripping. But then you can't ignore it, and it gets in your head. Unlike the apparitions, you can't make it go away. And it only happens further down."

"Are they...angry? Sad?" Ryan leaned forward. "Do you think they're trying to communicate?"

"Impossible to tell. It's like seeing something in your peripheral vision, always at the edge of your sight but never in focus. You can hear it, but you can't listen to it. It feels as if you could get just a little closer, or concentrate a little harder, you could make out the words. But it's always just out of reach."

Pete nodded. "There are other things. Too many to list. A lot of things happen only once, but we can't agree on exactly what it was. Once, I swore gravity stopped for a minute. Some of the others slipped and fell at the same time, but they didn't believe me."

Donavan added, "And one time at the water tank—"

Nathan flinched. Pete interrupted him. "We don't talk about that."

Donavan apologized, and turned to Ryan and Quinn. "It can get dangerous, but the danger is most always in your mind. Mostly."

"I think they're all connected somehow. All stemming from the same source. I don't know what or how, but this factory, or at least this section, doesn't belong to Devlin anymore. We're guests in something else's home. It doesn't seem hostile. As long as we keep to ourselves and leave it alone, I think we can all go home someday."

"Something else's home," Ryan mused. "Alex said almost the same thing. What was it exactly, Quinn?"

"'The destinies of the people Devlin abandoned have been inherited by something else,'" Quinn quoted. "His idea was that this thing, this source, is moving in as people move out. Like nature reclaiming land."

They nodded in agreement. "It makes as much sense as anything else I've heard."

"Why do you stay here? Can't you request a transfer?"

Nathan looked uneasy. "We all have contracts. Devlin avoids transfers unless you can negotiate it at the start of a new contract. A lower level employee might be able to sneak into a different department, or forge travel papers to a different city. But more valuable employees are often stuck where they are. Even if someone abandoned their post, there's no way they could make it across the border."

"Besides, this place isn't so bad." Pete leaned back in his chair. "Our jobs are important, and we get our pick of food and supplies."

"Yeah," Donavon added. "We don't get any fun supplies, but we already have mind-altering experiences. Could you imagine watching a power spike while high?"

"The work is simple and easy. As long as we do our jobs and turn in reports, there's no oversight. Some days we just watch the gauges and play video games." Blake picked his teeth with a fork.

Quinn perked up at the mention of video games. "Have you tried the new Blood War 3 yet?"

Blake leaned forward quickly. "I got it last week! Dude, it's so awesome! In the Dread Swamps-"

Quinn held up his hands. "Stop! I haven't played it yet. I was going to yesterday, but someone had different plans." He glared at Ryan. Ryan only shrugged apologetically.

Everyone else finished eating. Ryan pushed his empty plate away. "Thanks for the food. It was a lot better than what we brought. Where did you get it, anyway?"

"Every week, we get a helicopter shipment from the Tower. Food, water, entertainment, parts, and fuel for the generators. The next one is in a couple days."

"What are the generators for, anyway? Must be pretty important to station four people indefinitely."

"We're maintaining critical assets for the Tower. An archive. Full of sales data, I believe. The contents don't really matter to technicians."

Ryan and Quinn looked at each other. "What kind of archive? Is it paper or digital?"

"Digital, of course. Filing cabinets don't need generators."

Ryan stood up excitedly. "Is it a server room?"

Nathan was surprised at his outburst. "Yeah. We usually just call it the archive—"

Quinn stood up just as fast. "Can we see it?"

The server room was only a few meters away. As soon as it came into view, Quinn held up his tablet. "This is it! This is the server room!"

Even with the door closed, he could hear the whir of countless fans on the other side.

"What's going on?" Nathan asked. "What are you looking for?"

Ryan and Quinn looked at each other, and silently agreed to trust the other employees. They explained their objective in the server room.

The others shared their own look. "I don't know about phone maps," Nathan said. "We've never needed the phone system, but I don't see why we can't check."

Donovan pushed open the server room door. It wasn't locked. Inside were rows of old servers, with a jungle of wires and cables connecting them. Beyond that, piles of partially dismantled servers and equipment gathered dust in the corners. Shelves were overflowing with wires, keyboards, spare parts, and books. About two dozen filing cabinets crowded the remaining space.

It was difficult to talk in the noise, but the group spread out to look through the filing cabinets. It wasn't long before they found a dusty binder labeled "PBX". Inside were pages of aging documentation.

The employees took the binder to the server racks and compared numbers until they found the phone system. It was still powered on, unused for a decade or more. More numbers from the documentation showed which line went to extension 4985. It was still live.

The PBX documentation also included a map of the facility's phone lines. Carefully, they unfolded the map and marked the extension they were looking for.

Everyone walked out of the server room and shut the door. In the relative quiet, Quinn and Ryan placed the map on a table and stared at it.

"Well, there it is," Ryan said. "It's only a kilometer away. We just need to go to it."

"Are you actually thinking of going out there again?" Quinn asked incredulously. "The map we've used so far has been horribly wrong. How do we know this one is any different?"

Pete compared the phone map with his own. "The area where you got lost is to the west. We noticed the inconsistencies there as well. Your destination is to the east, and the maps have been accurate in that area so far. Even so, you could mark the walls with chalk in case you get lost."

Quinn rubbed his forehead. "Stop giving him ideas!"

"If you don't come back, the rescue team can use the chalk to find your bodies!"

"Thank you, Blake."

Ryan looked at the map thoughtfully. "We won't get another chance."

Quinn looked at Blake. "If you were Ryan, would you go?"

"Hmm. None of the anomalies actually seem to be hostile..."

Ryan agreed. "That's what I was thinking."

Nathan was looking at the map. "The phenomena mostly happens on the lower levels. We're on level four. The phone is located below level one."

"It's in the sublevels?"

"No, those are mostly access tunnels. This is different. I can't tell what." He looked at Quinn. "I wouldn't risk it, but it's up to you two."

"Go for it," Donovan said.

Pete shook his head.

Ryan studied the map some more, and turned to Quinn. "We came this far. I still think it's worth it."

"How is your leg?"

"I feel great!"

A horrible feeling of dread built up in Quinn, but he pushed it down. "Alright. Fine. Let's do this."

The outpost employees gave them supplies, another flashlight, and the map. Ryan wasn't sure if they were allowed to give it away, but they insisted it was useless to them. After a few hours rest, they set out again into the darkness.

At least they were right about the map. Their path was already laid out, and the stairwells were exactly where the map said they were. They confidently entered level one.

The flashlights faded once more, but they simply took a break with Quinn's lighter. The flashlight started working again after a few minutes.

No other anomalies appeared. No apparitions harassed them. There seemed to be nothing but emptiness in the cramped concrete labyrinth.

Their nervousness increased when they found the stairwell and went as far down as it would take them. But still nothing happened right away.

They walked for some time before they switched their flashlights off. They could see well enough without them.

Quinn stopped to read the map. His tablet wouldn't turn on, but the paper phone map had their route. There was just enough light to read. Ryan sat next to him, idly gazing into the darkness.

The accountant folded the map. "Come on, Ryan. Let's go."

"This is kind of weird, isn't it? Something's off."

"Of course it is."

"Hold on. Don't you have the chalk? Why aren't you marking the walls?"

Quinn pointed to the wall. "It's already marked. I even included the time."

Ryan examined the mark. "What time is it now?"

"It's still the same time." He marched on down the hall.

The salesman hurried after him. "Why aren't you more concerned?"

Quinn shrugged nonchalantly. "We're not lost, exactly. I can see where we are on the map. There are more concerning things. Like where the light is coming from."

Ryan looked around in panic. It was true. Without the flashlights they should be in total darkness. A dim, diffuse light permeated the walls. It seemed to come from the air itself.

"Don't wander," Quinn said.

"What are we going to do?"

"Keep walking."

"But we're going in circles! Look!" They passed by another chalk mark. The time was the still same.

"Not quite. Something is changing." As he spoke, the dim light slowly grew brighter. It took on a purple hue. But the objects around them didn't seem to be affected by the color or the brightness. In fact, they almost seemed to be fading.

Quinn blinked. The air was glowing now. A purplish fog drifted through the walls as if they weren't there. For all he knew, they really weren't.

"What's going on? What is this mist?" Ryan's voice seemed far away.

Quinn looked at his friend. "Alex said something is growing at the heart of the factory. We're at the very center." He pointed to the floor. "THIS is the heart."

Ryan looked terrified. "What if—"

"We had our chance to turn back. Now we can only go forward."

The walls in every direction seemed transparent, but there was nothing behind them except mist.

They walked in silence for a few minutes. Quinn turned to Ryan, but he was gone.

The factory had completely disappeared now. It seemed he could see for kilometers, but only clouds of mist met his gaze.

Quinn kept walking. Direction didn't seem to matter, only distance.

It could have been minutes or days later when he stopped again. The mist in front of him bubbled and oozed. A black liquid materialized and rose in front of him.

"Who are you to enter my domain?" The creature demanded. Its body was like an oil slick. Its voice was like a man gargling marbles underwater.

"I was just walking. It was you who brought me here."

"Liar! Why would I dirty my realm with your kind?"

"Why are you talking to me now? Why not send me on my way?"

"You presume to speak to me in such a manner? You are not fit to be my plaything!" It gargled menacingly.

"That's where I know you from!" Quinn pumped his fist in triumph. "The trailer from Blood War 3! You're one of the bosses!"

"You shall pay for your insolence!"

"If you could hurt me, you would have done it already. No, you're just another hallucination. Now, run along."

The oil slick stood menacingly. Bubbles slowly rose to the surface of its body and popped. It looked cool in the trailer, but now Quinn felt it was very silly.

Finally, it dissolved into the mist it came from. Quinn looked around expectantly.

Nothing met his eyes, but when he turned back around a woman was standing before him.

She was wearing robes that seemed to be light itself. Not purple, not even white, but the purest light imaginable. Her face was plain, but without blemish. Her blonde hair cascaded past her shoulders in thick ringlets. "What can I help you with?"

"Are you the being who lives here?"

She nodded once, almost amused. "I am."

"Do you mind if I ask a few questions?"

"Speak."

"What are you? Why are you here?"

She sat down with a flourish. A bench made of the same light had appeared behind her. Quinn found another for him, and he sat down as well.

"What I am, you could not understand. I exist outside your world, outside your science. As for my objective, my purpose...I have none. I am merely trying to survive."

"Survive what?"

She looked at him sadly. "Neither my dimension nor yours offer safety. Injustice and atrocities of nature and man abound. You could say I came seeking refuge, but I found only hardships of a different kind."

"But what about the phenomena? The apparitions and brownouts? Are you causing those?"

"I'm afraid side effects of my power may appear to those nearby. As I grow, that power expands ahead of me."

"Why are you growing? What do you need?"

She smiled. "All living things must grow or die. To escape my dimension, to fully integrate in your world, I must grow in your factory like a cancer."

Quinn frowned. "Cancers are bad."

"Of course."

"Why did you use that word? You could have said anything else."

The woman shrugged flippantly. "It came to mind."

"Why did you use that word?" Quinn was talking to himself now. The woman tossed her hair back and waited.

He looked at the woman. "It did come to mind. But not yours. That was the word *I* thought of." Quinn stood up. "In fact, this conversation has gone pretty much as I imagined it. You aren't any more real than Lord Sludge Oillous. You're just in my imagination."

The woman stood up and smiled. Her appearance shimmered like steam, and resolidified.

Quinn stared at a copy of himself.

"So," he began.

"So," his reflection replied.

"You're not really the thing living at the heart."

"I'm afraid not. Or rather, *you* are afraid not."

"Because you are literally my imagination."

Quinn's reflection hesitated. "Not just imagination. A mirror. I am a perfect duplicate of you."

"So you can't actually tell me anything I don't know."

"I can tell you what you already know, but refuse to believe."

"Alright. Let's start with all this." Quinn waved his hand to indicate everything around them. "What do I think it is?"

"You were close before, when you used the word 'cancer'. But that's not entirely true."

"As far as I know."

The reflection nodded. "As far as you know. And you were somewhat right when you thought this was outside science. Modern science has no understanding of what goes on here, but that doesn't mean there is no scientific explanation."

"That's what Alex said."

"Ultimately, Alex is the expert on these topics. But you are here at the heart. This is your discovery." The reflection collected his thoughts. "All these phenomena, you think they're connected. Everything originates from here. It's growing like a cancer, but cancers spread randomly. They attack even healthy organs. This thing lacks malice or intent of any kind, like a tumor, but it's not a cancer." He paused for effect. "It's an infection, growing in a wound."

"Yes! That's what I was trying to think of!" Quinn ran his fingers through his hair. "I thought this was alive, but it's not intelligent. And Alex thinks it was caused by the abandonment of the factory workers! It all makes sense! But how long will it last? Is it like a ghost that will dissipate once it completes unfinished business? Can we get rid of it?"

"Impossible to tell. You haven't found any evidence one way or another. But while this thing is dangerous, it's not actively hostile. The people still trapped here have bigger threats."

"Like what?"

The reflection thought for a moment. "This is like an infection, right? A wound wasn't treated properly. It was allowed to fester. This is probably just a minor infection. It won't actually kill the host, and they might develop an immunity before it gets serious. It's really more of an inconvenience for the patient at this point. The real problem is that the wound still isn't treated. And before the wound can heal, you need to remove the object that caused it. In this case, not only is the knife still in the wound, but the person who caused it is still holding the handle and twisting it inside."

Quinn frowned. "...Who's holding the knife? Devlin Incorporated?"

"Exactly. Whether by greed or carelessness, they abandoned not only these production lines but also the workers that ran them. Some were reassigned, some were fired, some were forced to take up the slack, and most were simply lost in the system. That is the great wound festering in the very fabric of this place."

"That can't be right."

Quinn's double shrugged. "That's what you believe. You could be wrong. But, it's not a bad guess. And between greed and incompetence, both scenarios are equally likely when dealing with the corporate world."

"As far as you know."

"As far as I know."

"There's still no evidence."

"And there may never be any. But whatever it is, whatever you find, know that this is not evil. You may see things that should be impossible, things that make you doubt your sanity. You may not be able to trust your senses. But that doesn't change your course of action."

"And what action is that?"

"To always do what you think is right. To question it, modify it, improve it, but never compromise it."

Quinn grimaced. "It's kind of a cheap answer after that dramatic build up."

"But you know it's the right answer."

"Yeah."

The mist swirled. No wind brushed his hair, but the purple fog danced in its own light.

"How long have we been here?"

"In this dreamscape? No time at all. In the factory? Impossible to say. There is no present in these ruins. Only a forgotten past, and an abandoned future."

"Tell me. What else do I know but refuse to believe?"

His reflection looked at him sadly. "This enterprise of Ryan's. It's doomed to fail."

"No! I don't believe that."

"Don't lie to yourself. This mission was unlikely to be successful from the start. You should have returned to the Tower the moment you found the first server room."

Quinn defended himself. "Yes, we've been through a lot. I wouldn't go through it again. But the end is in sight! We know where the phone is! We're close to our ultimate goal!"

"But do you know what desk it's on? Do you know if it even works? It could have been crushed, buried under a hundred meters of concrete. It's somewhere below level one. What will you find there? What horrors will find you?"

"Why are you telling me this?"

"You are telling yourself this. You're afraid, and you won't admit it. What good does the phone do, anyway? So Ryan gets his database. What if it's empty? What if all this was for nothing? What if you never get there, fated to wander this barren emptiness with only your own thoughts for all eternity?"

Quinn was silent. He had felt these thoughts the further he ventured into the factory, but every time he suggested turning around Ryan had insisted on going further. He had tried to be a good friend, and ignore his misgivings, but now they were being thrown back at him.

The reflection continued. "You're thinking about Ryan. About how all this was for him. About every warning you gave him, and how every time he ignored it and wandered further into this nightmare. What do you get out of it? He never promised you a cut. You assumed you would get one, but didn't want to barter. And here you are."

Quinn still said nothing.

"Ryan is gone. Vanished, dead, ran back to the Tower. You can't help him any more. When, if, you return to your world, what will you do if he doesn't return with you?" The reflection leaned in and whispered. "Or worse, what if he wants to keep going?"

Finally, Quinn spoke. "I won't leave him. I promised I wouldn't abandon him. I promised."

The reflection took a step back. "Is that the right thing to do?"

"It is. I have no doubt."

"Very well. You have made your decision, and decisions have consequences." The reflection stopped and listened to some distant, silent signal. "I also hope you are right. But for now, you need to wake up."

The mist was swept away by a sudden wind. Darkness swept in after it.

Quinn opened his eyes.

He was standing on a concrete platform four meters wide. Ryan was standing, wide eyed and just as confused, a meter to his left.

A single beam of light from the ceiling illuminated the platform, but not much else. Two metal walkways connected to the platform stretched off into the darkness in front and behind them. Massive pillars were barely visible to the sides, rising from the depths below and vanishing in the inky void above. Forward, backward, left, right, up, and down, nothing else could be seen.

Quinn turned to Ryan. "Are you okay?"

The salesman nodded. "I think so. Are you?"

"Yeah. Did you fall asleep on me?"

Ryan tried to remember. "I might have? I think I had a dream...It must have been a hallucination again."

"Mine was different. It was like a hallucination, but more like a lucid dream. I don't remember much. Oh, and Lord Sludge Oillous was in it."

"Awesome! I wish I could remember mine."

"Don't worry about it." Quinn took out his flashlight, but the tiny beam didn't reveal much more of the enormous space. "Any idea how we got here?"

"I was following you!"

"While sleepwalking. That doesn't bode well for our return trip." He shut off the flashlight. "Any ideas?"

"It looks like all we can do is follow a walkway until we find something."

"But which way?"

Ryan examined the walkways. What little he could see of them in the light was identical. "I suppose we shouldn't split up."

"No, that would be bad. Here's an idea!" Quinn took the flashlight and tapped the railing.

"What was that supposed to do?"

"Shh! Listen for the echo!"

Quinn tapped the railing again. Ryan heard an echo, but it seemed diffuse. "I think the pillars are interfering. Or maybe the walls aren't smooth."

"Maybe. Face ninety degrees, with your ears pointing at each walkway, and close your eyes." Quinn tapped again.

One echo did seem to return sooner than the rest. Ryan opened his eyes to see Quinn pointing.

"I agree. That's the nearest wall."

"The echo takes a little over a second to return...call it one and a quarter. Do you happen to know the speed of sound?"

"Not off the top of my head. Are you trying to calculate the distance?"

"Yeah. But it can't be that far." They turned on their flashlights and ventured into the dark.

It wasn't long before they found the wall. Great concrete pillars flanked doors of steel a meter thick, permanently propped open. Large, illegible symbols covered the doors. Flecks of paint that might have once been letters speckled the surface. Seeming very out of place, a placard with the words "Garret Headquarters" hung next to the entrance.

"We found it," said Ryan.

"This is the First Cold War bunker Carl told us about! Garret was here all along!"

"Why would Garret be set up in a place like this?"

"There were rumors their headquarters were bulldozed to build the factory. This must have been underneath, and they relocated here during construction. It was the height of the Second Cold War, after all, and the bunker must have seemed pretty attractive."

The corridor went straight in for five meters. "No wonder they decided to leave it intact. With this much reinforced concrete, it would take more than a nuke to demolish it."

Quinn unfolded the map. "The communications and power lines enter the facility from the north. From there, they branch to the network closets. The phone line for extension 4985 is...in office 62. Down two levels."

The architecture was almost a hundred years old. The concrete was cracked and crumbling in places, but it was built to survive nuclear blasts. A few decades of age would not weaken the ancient structure.

Most other places had been looted or trashed. Here, the offices were clean and the desks empty. No debris or rubble marred the oldest section in the factory.

At last, they stood before the desk in office 62. "4985" was clearly labeled on the faded telephone.

Solemnly, Quinn plugged his tablet into a network jack and opened the database. Ryan entered the password. Expectantly, they watched the telephone.

Moments passed in silence. Finally, the stillness was broken by ringing.

Ryan reached for the handset and picked it up.

A woman's voice cheerfully sounded from the speaker. It was tinny and filled with static, but he could hear "To complete your login, please press the pound key."

He pressed it. "Your login was successfully verified. Goodbye!" The phone disconnected.

"We're in! We have the database!"

Ryan rushed to the tablet. The login screen had been replaced by rows and rows of customer data. There must have been millions. "Yes! Now we just need to change the MFA number so we don't need to come back."

"I don't know, this place is kind of cozy. We could just move here."

"You can. I'm going back to the Tower."

"And abandon prime real estate? How many haunted hundred-year-old bunkers have you found lately?"

Ryan finished his task and handed the tablet back to Quinn. "No electricity for video games."

"Fine, we'll go back." They left the bunker.

The trip back was uneventful. The haunted section was just another empty, underground building. The only point of concern was a walkway over a deep shaft which had collapsed long ago. It was directly in their path.

An alternate route was nearby, but they could never have crossed the chasm while sleepwalking. It almost seemed as if they had been teleported to the entrance of the bunker.

They arrived at the outpost. It had been two days since they left, but it seemed like a few hours. Quinn confirmed the time on his tablet was wrong. Suspicious, but just one of those things that happens deep in the factory.

Rather than calling the executive helicopter and requesting an emergency extraction, they decided to hitch a ride on the supply helicopter. They climbed to the roof and waited.

The sky was gray. Clouds of smoke and smog obscured the cityscape. The roof was flat and featureless for kilometers in every direction. Somehow, despite the light, the wind, and the openness, it felt like they were still below.

The cargo helicopter wasn't as fast or comfortable as the corporate one, but there was room to lie down in. The Tower loomed ahead of them, a shining beacon of wealth and prosperity after the squalor of the factory. The light rain on their departure days ago had been replaced by columns of gray smog.

They landed, entered the shipping bay near the base of the tower, and took the elevator up to their living quarters. After a quick shower, it was difficult to believe the adventure they just had.

Ryan checked his voicemails online since he lost his phone. "Lots of missed calls from my manager. I should call him back."

Quinn glanced at the clock. "It's still business hours. Tim will be at his desk. Let's report in person."

They traveled to the sales department and walked to Tim's office. The door was closed.

Quinn hesitated, but Ryan knocked on the door. It opened a moment later.

"Well, if it isn't my little buddies!" James Gunn gleamed maniacally from the doorway. We were just talking about you! Come on in!" His tone of voice made it clear it wasn't a suggestion.

Tim sat behind the desk looking small and miserable. Ryan and Quinn took seats. "What's going on, Tim?"

James interrupted them. "You're late! You were supposed to be back four days ago! And you've only been gone four days! Can you see my dilemma?"

Quinn opened his mouth, but Ryan stopped him. "No, I really can't. You're not my manager. I don't report to you."

"You will soon! That's right. After your little stunt, your entire department will be reassigned to me!"

Tim's face went from misery to shock. Apparently this was the first he had heard of it.

James continued. "I've been waiting here for your return for days! You didn't check in, you didn't call the helicopter, for all we knew you were dead!" He stopped his tirade to catch his breath. "But it's not all bad. I saw someone managed to log in to the Legua database recently. That can only have been you. Now, hand it over."

"The database? It's on the network."

"The tablet, you idiot. I know you logged in on your tablet."

Quinn reluctantly gave up his tablet.

James tapped the screen. "It's logged out. No problem, I have the password...what?" Quinn smiled at his frustration. James put the tablet down and glared at him. "It's requesting a phone login! Did you two idiots forget to remove the phone requirement?"

Ryan started to reply, but James started yelling. "How could you be so dense? You went all that way to log in once, and didn't think you might need to log in after that? Were you going to have your entire department access the database through a tablet?"

Tim reached for the tablet while James continued his rant. His face displayed a mix of confusion and disappointment when he saw it was still calling XXX-XXX-XX85.

Ryan and Quinn shared a glance. They still had an ace, but for now it was best to let James believe what he wanted. James didn't seem to notice as he paced and shouted.

Finally, he ran out of breath. "You two...no, you three." He turned to point at Tim as well. "I should have realized you would be stupid enough to do something like this. Not only did you risk your lives in that lawless, barren wasteland, but you didn't even disable the Multi-Factor Authentication!" His voice started to pick up again. Quinn and Ryan resigned themselves to another shouting session. "Now, you might expect me to send you back there to do it correctly, and by all rights you deserve it! But I'm not stupid enough to let you get access to MY database for even another minute! No, I'll be sending my own team. When they get to that phone, I'll finally have what's mine, and you will all be working for me!" With that final shout, he slammed the door open and marched out of the office. He narrowly missed Fred about to knock on the door.

Fred ducked to cover his face, but James didn't seem to notice him. "Wow, what's his problem?" Fred closed the door behind him. "No, I'm just kidding. I know what his problem is."

Tim narrowed his eyes. "Aren't you in IT? What are you doing here?"

"Yes. I helped Quinn get the information. When I saw his cellphone connect to the wifi I knew he was back in the Tower."

"And you knew I was here because...?"

Fred turned to Quinn and pointed at the wifi antenna on the ceiling of Tim's office. "Because this is the nearest hotspot to your phone. I came to tell you James was looking for you, but I see he already found you. Sorry about that."

Quinn was incredulous. "You can track my movements that precisely?"

"In the tower, yeah. We have great network technology. Wait, did you not know that?"

Ryan interrupted. "Never mind that. How did you know James was looking for us? And how did James know what we were doing?"

Tim only shrugged. In the rollercoaster of events, he still had not uttered a word. Fred looked ashamed. "Yeah, he asked me what you were doing. He tried to intimidate me. I felt bad afterwards and tried to warn you, but I couldn't reach your cell. You must have already been inside the factory."

"Uh huh." Quinn was unconvinced.

"Anyway, after my conversation with James, I discovered what you were after. I figured I was better off helping you. I don't need a cut. I'm satisfied with putting James down." He shrugged. "A bonus would be nice, though."

Tim finally spoke. "It doesn't matter. We didn't get it. James will have the database, and there's nothing we can do about it. Unless you two know differently...?"

Ryan smiled. "As a matter of fact, we do!"

"Hold on," Quinn said. "I don't think we can trust Fred right now."

Fred lifted his hands in surrender. "I get it. I sold you out. But after spending an hour with James, I want to see that jerk go down too. You owe me one." He opened the door behind him and left.

The only ones in the office were Ryan, Quinn, and Tim.

"Where were we?" Quinn asked. He took out his phone.

"We were just about to explain our genius plan to Tim. Do you have a missed call, Quinn?"

"I do indeed. I'm glad I put it on silent before we came. It would have been awkward to have it go off while James was here."

Tim spoke up. "Okay, what's your genius plan?"

Ryan smiled. "Obviously, we weren't going to just remove the phone requirement from the database. We were the first to reach the phone, but we might not have been the first to find the password. Someone like James could have been watching and opened it before we even got back. We were thinking of which phone number we could change it to, when we realized Quinn's cellphone number also ends in 85. No one would even realize it had been changed. That's why we didn't change the password yet."

"So, we can log in to the database?"

Ryan motioned to Tim's computer. "Go ahead."

He entered the password, and Quinn's cellphone rang to verify. Tim looked in approval at the rows of customers.

"We have a lot of work ahead of us, but the hard part is over. Hopefully, we can get a lot done before James realizes he's been had. Thank you, both of you."

Ryan and Quinn went back to their apartment.

"It's finally over." Ryan collapsed on a chair. "We won."

Quinn nodded. He sat on the couch. "Yeah, unless James has something else up his sleeve. Probably not, though."

"What if he gets to the phone in the Garret headquarters and discovers it's been changed?"

"I don't think he'll get that far. Even if he asked the people at the outpost, we have the only physical phone line map." He patted his backpack. "By the time he figures it out, you'll already be making such a profit that you and Tim will be untouchable."

Ryan leaned back in his chair. "I guess so. But won't James be surprised when he sees the ghosts? And the flooded section. I would love to see his face when he thinks he's about to be eaten by a tentacle monster!"

"Yeah, me too. But he'll just bribe someone to send a security team instead. And it sounds like he won't be that surprised. He called the factory a 'lawless, barren wasteland'. It seems he already knows some of what's going on there."

"What? How is that possible? He would never set foot outside the Tower."

"He's always bragging about his friends in upper management. If I had to guess, I'd say he heard it from them."

"But...that means they already know." Ryan slumped into the cushions. "All those people. Curtis, and Mary. The Tower really left them trapped down there? And they aren't doing anything to rescue them?"

Quinn was silent for a while. "Between greed and incompetence, both scenarios are equally likely."

"Yeah. Where did you hear that?"

"My subconscious told me, while we were sleepwalking."

"I wish my subconscious was as witty as yours. I mostly had an infinite loop of 'Never Gonna Give You Up.'" Ryan was silent for a while. "Quinn?"

"Yeah?"

"It's easy to ignore some of the things we saw down there. The monster in the water was a hallucination caused by mold spores, sure. And the things in the basement could just be bats. The trouble in the shaft was caused by a random power spike. And we were seeing things when the ghosts appeared. If that was all, I could have just walked away without a second thought. But how did we move from the outpost to the bunker? Where were we for two days? We both woke up at the same time, standing upright. I didn't feel as if I had been walking for forty eight hours."

"Not only that, but the time on my tablet and cellphone both was off by two days. Physically, it's as if we weren't there." Quinn thought for a few moments. "Another thing my subconscious said: 'There is no present in these ruins. Only a forgotten past, and an abandoned future.' I'm starting to remember some more. I'm not sure it was a dream, anymore. The person I was talking to acted like my subconscious. It certainly knew my thoughts. But sometimes it seemed to know too much. And at the end, it told me 'it was time to wake up'. As if it knew where I was in the factory."

Ryan leaned forward. "Do you think you were actually talking to the source?"

Quinn frowned. "No idea. Nothing makes sense. But I think it gave me a warning. The real problem isn't whatever is happening in the abandoned sections. The global economy is a cutthroat arena for megacorporations. The rest of us, the actual workers, are merely collateral damage. The cost of doing business. Garret Plastics used to be one of the top manufacturers in the global economy, and now their headquarters lies at the bottom of an empty factory."

It took Ryan a few seconds to figure out his meaning. "You think the same thing could happen here? That's impossible. Devlin is the biggest producer of...hmm."

Quinn took out his cellphone and placed it on the table. "The database login is still attached to my number. What if we heard Devlin was being bought out today, this very minute. And for some reason, the new owners were moving everyone immediately."

"That's absurd," Ryan said, as his face tightened.

"My cellphone, still on the table. I didn't have time to grab it. Twenty years from now, some other desk jockey needs access to the Legua database. They have to trek through the abandoned Tower trying to find this exact room. Who knows what they'll find?"

"It's not possible."

"And yet, it's happened before." Quinn gazed at his cellphone thoughtfully. "It could happen again."

"Okay, now you're making me nervous. Put your phone back in your pocket before Devlin gets bought out."

Quinn grabbed his cellphone and smiled. "The world is a harsh place. There's a lot of ways people on the bottom can get lost and forgotten. But today, we won. Today, we celebrate." He lifted the couch cushion he was sitting on and pulled out his copy of Blood War 3. "Let's murder digital monsters."

Two months later, the Legua database was starting to show some results. Not nearly as much as Tim estimated, but still enough for management to notice. James noticed too, but there wasn't much he could do about it. Fred was willing to keep an eye on him, and alerted Ryan whenever James was trying something underhanded. It seemed there was no end to his bullying, but Ryan, Quinn, and Tim were satisfied with keeping the database from him.

To officially celebrate their success, Tim organized a dinner for everyone. Alex, Fred, Carl the helicopter pilot, and even Nathan from the outpost were invited. He was rotated back to the Tower for six months, and was having trouble adjusting to society. Everyone had a good time. Most of the night was spent listening to Alex and Carl swap stories.

Quinn and Ryan filed dozens of reports. Fred tracked their progress up the chain of command, watching each of them get rejected until he found a pattern. The three of them carefully organized a report which reached the least corrupt managers and exposed the conditions in the Garret-Lasanko factory. The building was condemned later that year. The inhabitants were forced to move out. Alex knew they didn't find everyone. Rumors circulated of corrupt middle-managers who refused the order to evacuate and hid inside. Once the power was shut off, it didn't matter. The entrances were sealed and the structure left to decay.

The thing at the heart of the factory was never investigated. Officially, it didn't exist. The former squatters swore it was haunted. But deep down, through the layers of concrete and stale air, it festered. It grew slowly, taking its time in the completely abandoned structure. Thoughts, memories, and emotions left frozen in time from the evacuees became fuel for the smoldering expanse. It was unfettered in the darkness, and grew to consume everything. Only the flickering torchlight from handfuls of survivors kept it at bay. But soon, it would fill the factory. Soon, it would reach out and find new homes. There were other wounds in society waiting to be filled. To be infected.

Soon.

All characters, corporations, and entities in this story are fictional and have no relation to existing characters, corporations, or entities. Except Alex.